3 4028 07181 1922
HARRIS COUNTY PUBLIC LIBRARY
W9-AKD-303
LAP

WOODS RUNNER

Also by Gary Paulsen

Alida's Song • *The Amazing Life of Birds* • *The Beet Fields*
The Boy Who Owned the School
The Brian Books: *The River, Brian's Winter, Brian's Return,* and *Brian's Hunt*
Canyons • *Caught by the Sea: My Life on Boats*
The Cookcamp • *The Crossing*
Danger on Midnight River • *Dogsong*
Father Water, Mother Woods • *The Glass Café*
Guts: The True Stories Behind Hatchet *and the Brian Books*
Harris and Me • *Hatchet*
The Haymeadow • *How Angel Peterson Got His Name*
The Island • *Lawn Boy* • *The Legend of Bass Reeves*
Molly McGinty Has a Really Good Day
The Monument • *Mudshark* • *My Life in Dog Years*
Nightjohn • *The Night the White Deer Died*
Notes from the Dog
Puppies, Dogs, and Blue Northers
The Quilt • *The Rifle*
Sarny: A Life Remembered • *The Schernoff Discoveries*
Soldier's Heart • *The Time Hackers* • *The Transall Saga*
Tucket's Travels (the Tucket's West series, Books One through Five)
The Voyage of the Frog • *The White Fox Chronicles* • *The Winter Room*

Picture books, illustrated by Ruth Wright Paulsen:
Canoe Days and *Dogteam*

GARY PAULSEN

WOODS RUNNER

This is a work of fiction. Names, characters, places, and incidents either are the product of the author's imagination or are used fictitiously. Any resemblance to actual persons, living or dead, events, or locales is entirely coincidental.

 Published in the United States by Wendy Lamb Books, an imprint of Random House Children's Books, a division of Random House, Inc., New York.

Wendy Lamb Books and the colophon are trademarks of Random House, Inc.

Visit us on the Web! www.randomhouse.com/teens
Educators and librarians, for a variety of teaching tools, visit us at www.randomhouse.com/teachers

Library of Congress Cataloging-in-Publication Data
Paulsen, Gary.
Woods runner / Gary Paulsen. — 1st ed.
p. cm.
Summary: From his 1776 Pennsylvania homestead, thirteen-year-old Samuel, who is a highly-skilled woodsman, sets out toward New York City to rescue his parents from the band of British soldiers and Indians who kidnapped them after slaughtering most of their community. Includes historical notes.
ISBN 978-0-385-73884-2 (hc) — ISBN 978-0-385-90751-4 (lib. bdg.) — ISBN 978-0-375-85908-3 (pbk.) — ISBN 978-0-375-89634-7 (ebook)
[1. Kidnapping—Fiction. 2. Frontier and pioneer life—Pennsylvania—Fiction. 3. Soldiers—Fiction. 4. Espionage—Fiction. 5. Indians of North America—Pennsylvania—Fiction. 6. Pennsylvania—History—Revolution, 1775–1783—Fiction. 7. United States—History—Revolution, 1775–1783—Fiction.]
I. Title.
PZ7.P2843Woo 2010 [Fic]—dc22 2009027397

The text of this book is set in 12.5-point Adobe Garamond.
Book design by Vikki Sheatsley

Printed in the United States of America
10 9 8 7 6 5 4 3 2 1
First Edition

With appreciation, for Shelby

Author's Note

I've written this book a bit differently from my other historical fiction, alternating the fiction with historical segments that I feel are essential for the reader. I did this for two reasons. One: I wanted to set Samuel's story against the larger context of the Revolutionary War. And two: I wanted readers to understand what it was really like to live on the frontier at that time, with virtually nothing—no money, no electricity, no towns, few neighbors—nothing but your own strength.

Contents

PART 1

GREEN
The Forest—1776

CHAPTER 1

He was not sure exactly when he became a child of the forest.

One day it seemed he was eleven and playing in the dirt around the cabin or helping with chores, and the next, he was thirteen, carrying a .40-caliber Pennsylvania flintlock rifle, wearing smoked-buckskin clothing and moccasins, moving through the woods like a knife through water while he tracked deer to bring home to the cabin for meat.

He sat now by a game trail waiting for the deer he knew would come soon. He had heard it, a branch brushing a hairy side, a twig cracking, smelled it when the wind blew toward him, the musk and urine of a buck. He checked the priming on his rifle while he waited, his mind and body relaxed, patient, ears and eyes and nose alert. Quiet. Every part of him at rest, yet focused and intense.

And he pictured his life, how he lived in two worlds.

Sometimes Samuel thought that a line dividing those worlds went right through their cabin. To the west, beyond the small parchment window made of grease-soaked sheepskin scraped paper-thin, lay the forest.

The forest was unimaginably vast, impenetrable, mysterious and dark. His father had told him that a man could walk west for a month, walk as fast as he could, and never see the sun, so high and dense was the canopy of leaves.

Even close to their homestead—twelve acres clawed out of the timber with a small log cabin and a lean-to for a barn—the forest was so thick that in the summer Samuel could not see more than ten or fifteen yards into it. Some oak and elm and maple trees were four and five feet in diameter and so tall and thickly foliaged their height could only be guessed.

A wild world.

And while there were trails made by game and sometimes used by natives, settlers or trappers, the paths wandered and meandered so that they were impossible to use in any sensible way. Except to hunt.

When he first started going into the forest, Samuel went only a short distance. That first time, though he was well armed with his light Pennsylvania rifle and dry powder and a good knife, he instantly felt that he was in an alien world.

As a human he did not belong. It was a world that did not care about man any more than it cared about dirt, or grass, or leaves. He did not get lost that first time, because he'd marked trees with his knife as he walked so he could find his way out; but still, in some way he felt lost, as if, were he not careful, a part of him would disappear and never return, gone to the wildness. Samuel had heard stories of that happening to some men. They entered the forest to hunt or trap or look for new land to settle and simply vanished.

"Gone to the woods," people said of them.

Some, he knew, were dead. Killed by accident, or panthers or bear or Indians. He had seen such bodies. One, a man mauled to death by a bear that had attacked his horse while the man was plowing; the man's head was eaten; another, killed by an arrow through the throat. An arrow, Samuel knew, that came out of the woods from a bow that was never seen, shot by a man who was never known. And when he was small, safe inside the cabin near the mud-brick fireplace with his mother and father, he had heard the panthers scream; they sounded like a woman gone mad.

Oh, he knew the forest could kill. Once, sitting by the fire, a distant relative, a shirttail uncle who was a very old man of nearly fifty named Ishmael, had looked over his shoulder as if expecting to see monsters and said, "Nothing dies of old age in the forest. Not bugs, not deer, not bear nor panthers nor man. Live long enough, be slow enough, get old enough and something eats you. Everything kills."

And yet Samuel loved the forest now. He knew the sounds and smells and images like he knew his own mind, his own yard. Each time he had entered he'd gone farther, learned more, marked more trees with his knife, until he always *knew* where he was. Now he thought of the deep forest as his home, as much as their cabin.

But some men vanished for other reasons, too. Because the forest pulled them and the wild would not let them go. Three years ago, when Samuel was ten, he had seen one of these men, a man who moved like smoke, his rifle a part of his arm, a tomahawk through his belt next to a slab-bladed knife, eyes that saw all things, ears that heard all things. One family in the settlement had a room on their cabin that was a kind of store. The man had come to the store to buy small bits of cloth and powder and English flints for his rifle at the same time Samuel was waiting for his mother to buy thread.

The man smelled of deep forest, of smoke and blood and grease and something green—Samuel knew he smelled that way, too. The stranger could not be still. As he stood waiting, he moved. Though he was courteous and nodded to people, as soon as he had the supplies for his rifle and some salt, he left. He was there one moment and gone the next, into the trees, gliding on soft moccasins to become part of the forest, as much as any tree or leaf or animal. He went west.

Away from man, away from the buildings and the settled land.

Now Samuel heard a new sound. He moved his eyes slowly to the left without turning his head and was rewarded by seeing a tick-infested rabbit sitting by a tree trying to clear the insects out of his ears. Samuel smiled. Even in dead of winter the rabbits were always trying to rid themselves of the pests.

The sight made him think of his mother, who was intensely curious and had once asked him to take her into the forest. They had not gone far, not over five hundred yards from the edge of the clearing, and had stopped under a towering oak where sunlight could not get through. There was a subdued green light over everything. Even their faces looked a gentle green.

"I have to go back," she said, her eyes wide, wrapping a shawl tightly around her shoulders, though it was summer-warm. "This is too . . . too . . . thick. Even the air is green. So thick it feels like it could be cut. I have to go back now."

Although Samuel's parents lived in the wilderness, they were not a part of it. They had been raised in towns and had been educated in schools where they'd been taught to read and write and play musical instruments. They moved west when Samuel was a baby, so that they could devote themselves to a quiet life of hard physical work and contemplation. They loved the woods, but they did not understand them. Not like Samuel.

They had told their son that they didn't belong in towns, either. They weren't comfortable in the world of roads, houses and villages. East of the imaginary line in the cabin was what his father and mother called civilization.

They told Samuel about the chaos of towns that they'd

escaped. There were noises—hammers clanging at blacksmith forges, chickens clucking, dogs barking, cows lowing, horses whinnying and whickering, people who always seemed to need to be talking to one another.

There wasn't noise in the forest.

There were smells: wood smoke filled the air in every season because it wasn't just for heat, but to cook as well; the smell of oak for long fires, pine for short and fast and hot fires. The smell of bread, and sometimes, if they were lucky and had honey or rock sugar to pulverize in a sack with a hammer, sweet pie. The odor of stew cooking in the cast-iron pot over an outside fire or in an iron kettle hung in the fireplace, the scent flying up through the chimney and out over the ground as the wind moved the smoke around. There was the tang of manure, stacked in back of small shedlike barns to age before it was put on gardens; horse and cow and chicken manure from their farm and other farms. So many smells swirled by the same wind throughout the small valley.

Their valley was like a huge bowl, nestled in the hills in far western Pennsylvania. Here lived, and had always lived, Samuel Lehi Smith, age thirteen, with his father, Olin, and his mother, Abigail, parents whom Samuel did not always understand but whom he loved.

They read to him about the world beyond from their prized books. All the long winter nights with tallow candles burning while they sat by the fireplace, they read aloud to each other. At first he'd listened as they took turns. Later he read to himself and knew the joyous romp of words on paper. He read all the books they had in the cabin and then books from other cabins in the valley so that he could know more and more of a world found only in his imagination and dreams.

To the east lay the faraway world of enormous cities and the Great Sea and Europe and Ancient Rome and Darkest Africa and the mysterious land of the Asias and so many people they couldn't be counted. All kinds of different people with foreign languages and their knowledge of strange worlds.

To the east lay polished shoes and ornate clothes and formal manners and enormous wealth. His mother would spin tales for him about cultured men who wore carefully powdered wigs and dipped snuff out of little silver snuffboxes and beautiful women dressed in gowns of silk and satin with swirling petticoats as they danced in the great houses and exclusive salons of London and Paris.

Now. The deer stepped out. It stood in complete profile not thirty yards away. Samuel held his breath. He waited for it to turn away, look around in caution. When it did, he raised the rifle and cocked the hammer, pulling it back as quietly as he could, the sear dropping in with a soft *snick.* The rifle had two triggers, a "set" trigger that armed a second, front trigger and made it so sensitive that a mere brush released the hammer. He moved his finger from the set trigger and laid it next to but didn't touch the hair trigger. Then he settled the German silver blade of the front sight into the tiny notch of the rear sight and floated the tip of the blade sight until it rested just below the shoulder of the young buck.

Directly over its heart.

A half second, no, a quarter second passed. Samuel could touch the hair trigger now and the hammer would drop, the flint would scrape the metal "frizzen," kicking it out of the way and showering sparks down on the powder in the small pan, which would ignite and blow a hot jet of gas into the touch hole on the side of the barrel of the rifle, setting off the charge, propelling the small .40-caliber ball down the bore. Before the buck heard the sound of the rifle, the ball would pass through the heart and out the other side of the deer, killing it.

And yet he did not pull the trigger. He waited. Part of a second, then a full second. And another. The deer turned, saw him standing there. With a convulsive explosion of muscle, it jumped straight in the air. It landed running and disappeared into the trees.

The whole time Samuel had not really been thinking of the deer, but what lay east. Of what they called civilization. He eased the hammer of the rifle down to the first notch on the sear, a safety position, and lowered the weapon. Oddly, he wasn't disappointed that he'd not taken the deer, though the fresh meat would have been nice roasted over the hearth. He'd killed plenty of deer, sometimes ten or fifteen a day, so many they could not possibly eat all the meat. He often shot them because the deer raided the cornfields and had to be killed to save the crops. Most families did not like deer meat anyway. They considered it stringy and tough and it was often wormy. The preferred meat was bear or beaver, which were richer and less "cordy."

This deer would have been nice. They had not had fresh meat in nearly two weeks. But it was gone now.

He could not stop his wondering about what lay to the east. The World. It was supposed to be a better place than the frontier, with a more sensible way to live. And yet he had just learned an ugly truth about that world only the evening before.

Those people in the world who were supposed to be civilized, full of knowledge and wisdom and graciousness and wealth and education, were caught in the madness of vicious, bloody war.

It did not make any sense.

Samuel started trotting back toward the cabin in an easy shuffle-walk that moved him quietly and at some speed without wearing out his moccasins; he was lucky to get a month per pair before they wore through at the heels.

He moved without a great deal of effort, his eyes and ears missing very little as he almost flowed through the forest.

But his mind was still on the man who had brought the sheet of paper the night before.

Communication

In the year 1776, the fastest form of travel for any distance over thirty or forty miles was by ship. With steady wind, a sailing vessel could clock one to two hundred miles a day for weeks on end.

A horse could cover thirty, maybe even forty, miles a day, although not for an extended period without breaking down.

At best, coaches could do a hundred miles in a twenty-four-hour day by changing horses every ten or fifteen miles, but only if the roads were in good shape, which they almost never were.

A man could walk twenty or thirty miles a day—faster for short periods, but always depending on conditions of land, weather and footgear. Fifteen miles a day was standard.

So there was no fast and dependable way to transmit information in those years—no telegraph, no telephone, no Internet, no texting, no overnight delivery services.

It might take five or six days for knowledge of an important event to move just ten miles, carried by a traveler on foot. Settlements were twelve to fifteen miles apart. And information was carried by hand from person to person on paper or, in most cases, shared by word of mouth.

CHAPTER 2

Samuel had returned home from the forest the night before and found his parents sipping tea with Isaac, an old man of the forest who stopped by their cabin every few months while he was hunting. This time, though, he had news. He carried information about a fight in Lexington and Concord, Massachusetts, where militia had fired on and defeated British soldiers. The battle had happened months before, all the way back in April of 1775.

Isaac seemed to be made entirely of scraps of old leather and rags. He was bald and wore a ratty cap with patches of fur that had been worn away. He was tall and thin and for many years had lived in a cabin some twenty miles to the east. He was so much a part of the forest that even his brief visits with Samuel's family caused him discomfort.

He'd decided to move farther into the frontier when a wagon, pulled by oxen, came into the clearing near his cabin. The family was traveling westward, looking for a piece of land to farm, and had chosen a spot not far from Isaac's place.

The family was, Isaac said, "a crowd. And I knew it was time to move on, seeing as how I don't do particular good with crowds of people."

As he was taking his leave from the small shack where he had lived, the family had given him the scrap of paper, soft with wear from all the hands it had passed through, so he could share the news with fellow travelers he met on his journey. They told him of other events they had heard of along the way. He tried to remember the details, but admitted that he wasn't much for conversation.

"Since they was so much noise from the sprats as it seemed a dozen of them, my thinker fuzzed up like bad powder and my recollecter might not be all it could be, but I think they said they was another fight at a place called Bunker Hill and the patriot militia got whipped there and sent running when they saw the bayonets on the British soldiers' muskets."

He sat, quietly sipping the evergreen tea he always carried, a brew made from pine and spruce needles. He swore it cured colds, and he said he preferred it over "furriner tea from outside, but thankee, missus."

The paper he'd handed to Samuel's father, Olin, was a single sheet that had been folded and unfolded so many times it was near to falling apart. It had been printed on a crude press with wooden block letters and was smudged and hard to read. But there was a brief description of the fight at Lexington and Concord and a drawing of figures firing muskets at some other figures that were falling to the ground.

As Samuel studied the paper in his father's hands, he thought: Everything in my world just got bigger.

Two other families, the Clarks and the Overtons, pulled up in wagons. Isaac had spoken to them on his way to Samuel's place and they wanted to hear what Olin had to say about Isaac's news.

Samuel looked around the small cabin on the edge of the woods that was suddenly filled with people all talking over each other about the meaning of the battles. It seemed that the strong and sturdy log walls no longer protected his family. The loud outside world his parents had escaped by moving to the frontier had found them. Samuel was excited and frightened and overwhelmed all at the same time.

"What does it mean?" Ebenezer Clark asked Olin. His face was red and round as an apple because he drank home beer, three quarts every morning for breakfast.

"It could be local. Just some trouble in Boston," Samuel's father said. "A riot or the like. There's always a chance of rabble-rousing in the cities. And it doesn't seem likely that a group of farmers would try to take on the entire British army." He paused, then added thoughtfully, "England has the most powerful army and navy in the world, and a gaggle of farmers would have to be insane to fight them."

"Likely or not"—this from Lund Harris, a soft-spoken and careful man whose wife, Clara, sat nursing an infant—"if it happens, we have to think what it means for us out here on the edge."

Nobody spoke. Samuel could hear the crackle of the fire in the fireplace. In the homey, safe cabin, the craziness of the information from the east seemed impossible.

There was always some measure of violence on the frontier: marauding savages, drunks, thieves—"evildoers," men who operated outside the walls of reason. Harshness was to be expected in the wild.

But nothing like this, nothing that challenged the established order, the very rule of the Crown, the civilized life that came from the English way of living.

The very idea of fighting the British was too big to understand, too huge to even contemplate. These settlers had always been loyal to the rules of the land, obedient to the laws of the country that ruled them.

Ben Overton stood. He was a tall, thin man whose sleeves never seemed to come to his wrists. He said, "Well, I think we should do nothing but wait and see how the wind blows."

And with nods and a few mumbles of affirmation the rest got up and went back to their own homes.

Not a single person in that cabin could have known what was coming. And even if they had seen the future, they would not have been able to imagine the horror.

Frontier Life

The only thing that came easy to people of the frontier was land. A single family could own hundreds, even thousands of acres simply by claiming them.

If getting the land was easily accomplished, using the land was a different matter. It had to be cleared of trees for farming. Some oaks were five or six feet in diameter, and each had to be chopped down by ax, cut into manageable sections and hauled off. Then the stump was dug out of the ground, often with a handmade wooden shovel. One stump might take a week or two of hard work, and a piece of land could have tens of dozens of trees.

If a family was lucky they might find a clearing left by beavers, which log off an area and dam a creek to make a lake, rotting out all the stumps. When the trees and the food are gone, the beavers leave, the dam breaks down, the water drains off and there is a handy clearing left where the lake was.

CHAPTER 3

The woods were never completely quiet.

Even in silence, there would be a whisper, a soft change that told something. If you listened, complete quiet could speak worlds.

Samuel had gone five ridges away from home, hunting, feeling the woods. Something was . . . off. If not wrong, then different. The woods felt strange, as if something had changed or was about to change.

Samuel shrugged off the feeling and kept going. It was hard to measure distance, because the ridges varied in height and width and the forest canopy blocked out the sun. He was hunting bear, so he moved slowly and followed the aimless game trails looking for signs of life.

Five ridges, going in a straight line, might have meant

four or five miles. The wandering path he followed probably covered more like seven or eight.

He had seen no fresh sign until he came halfway up the fifth ridge, a thickly forested round hump shaped like the back of a giant animal. Then he saw fresh bear droppings, still steaming, filled with berry seeds and grass stems, and he slowed his pace through the thick undergrowth until he came to the top of the ridge. To his surprise, the trees were gone, and he could see miles in all directions.

He had hunted this direction many times, but had never reached this ridge before. The thick undergrowth in the summer and early fall had kept him from seeing this high point. He was amazed to find that below him on the western side of the ridge lay a small valley perhaps half a mile long and a quarter mile wide. The graceful chain of round meadows and lush grass was already perfect farmland. The treeless patch just needed rail fencing and a cabin to be complete.

"Perfect," he said aloud. "Like it was made to be used."

A crunching noise to his rear, to the east, brought him around. The bear was forty or so yards away, a yearling, slope-shouldered, dark brown more than black. Like a large dog, it was digging in a rotten stump on the edge of the clearing. Samuel cocked his rifle, raised it and then held. He looked above the bear across the tops of trees.

Smoke.

Thick clouds of smoke were rising to the east, almost straight to the east, a goodly distance away. Forest fire? But it wasn't that dry and there had been no thunderstorms, the normal cause of forest fires.

Then he remembered that their neighbor Overton was going to burn limbs and brush from trees he had felled and cleared. The direction and distance looked about right for the settlement.

The bear moved, stood and looked at him, then dropped and was gone without Samuel's firing. Another missed kill.

The smoke was in the right direction and at the probable distance, but there was something wrong with it, the way there had been something wrong with the feel of the woods today.

He eased the hammer down on his rifle and lowered the butt to the ground. He stood leaning on it, studying the smoke the way he would read sign from a wounded animal, trying to see the "why" of it.

The gray smudge was wide, not just at the base but as it rose up, too wide for a single pile of slash. That could be explained by wind blowing the smoke around.

But it was a still, clear day.

All right, he thought, so Overton set fire to the slash and it spread into some grass and that made it wider. But the grass in the settlement area had been grazed to the ground by the livestock and what was left was still green and hard to burn.

And would not make a wide smoke.

Would not make such a dark, wide smoke that it could be seen from . . . how far?

Maybe eight miles?

Smoke that would show that dark and that wide from eight miles away on a clear, windless day had to be intentional.

He frowned, looking at the smoke, willing it to not be what was coming into his mind like a dark snake, a slithering horror. Some kind of attack. No. He shook his head.

No.

There had been years of peace. Even with a war, a real war, starting back east in the towns and cities, it would not have come out here so soon; it had only been a week since they'd heard the news.

It could not come this soon.

But even as he thought this, his mind was calculating. Distance home: eight miles in thick forest. Time until dark: an hour, hour and a half. No moon: it would be hard dark.

Could he run eight miles an hour through the woods in the dark?

It would be like running blind.

An attack.

Had there been an attack on the settlement, on his home?

He started running down the side of the ridge. Not a crazy run, but working low and slipping into the game trails, automatically looking for a turn or shift that would take him more directly home.

Home.

An attack on his home.

An attack on his mother and father?

And he had not been there to help.

Deep breaths, hard, and deep pulls of air as he increased his speed, moccasins slapping the ground, rifle held out in front of him to move limbs out of the way as he loped through the forest. The green thickness that once helped him now seemed to clutch at him, pull him back, hold him.

An attack.

And he had not been there to protect his parents.

PART 2

Red

War—1776

Weapons

A single rifle—something every frontier family needed, something that was an absolute necessity—might take a year or more, and a year's wages, to get from one of the rare gunsmiths, located perhaps miles away.

This was the only weapon many of the rebels carried into battle against the British.

The firearm issued to the British army was called the Brown Bess musket. It was a smoothbore and fired a round ball of .75 caliber, approximately three-quarters of an inch in diameter, with a black-powder charge, ignited by flint, that pushed the ball at seven or eight hundred feet per second when it left the muzzle (modern rifles send the bullet out at just over three thousand feet per second).

Because a round ball fired from a smoothbore is so pitifully inaccurate—the ball bounces off the side of the bore as it progresses down the barrel—the Brown Bess was really only good out to about fifty yards. The ball would vary in flight so widely that it was common for a soldier to aim at one man coming at him and hit another man four feet to the left or right.

With the Brown Bess, each British soldier was issued a bayonet, nearly three feet long, that twist-locked to the end of the barrel and turned the empty weapon into a kind of attacking pike.

Along with personal weapons, the British army employed artillery, small field cannon, which fired plain round balls, exploding shells and grapeshot: scores of round musket balls packed down the bore to make the cannon into something like a giant shotgun. Grapeshot was so viciously effective against columns of marching men that its destruction would not be duplicated until the use of the rapid-fire machine gun in the First World War. Whole ranks of attacking men could be torn to pieces in a single shot, the musket ball passing through man after man, ripping them apart.

CHAPTER 4

Samuel smelled it before he saw anything.

Not just the smoke from the fires. But the thick, heavy smell. Blood. Death.

No.

The single word took over his brain. Part of his thinking was automatic, leading him to act with caution, move with stealth. But the front part, the thinking part, hung on one word.

No.

He'd made good time, running hard until his lungs seemed to be on fire, then jogging until he got his breath, then back to the full-out run. There was probably another half hour of daylight before it was too dark to see. As he approached the settlement he slowed and moved off to the side. It would do no good to run head-on if the attackers were still there.

He was silent, listening keenly. Surely if anyone was still there they would make some noise. All Samuel heard was the crackling of fire, the soft night sounds of evening birds.

No human sound.

At the edge of the clearing near his home he paused, frightened, no, terrified at what he would find. He was hidden in some branches and he studied the area through the leaves to make sure it was clear before he stepped out.

The cabin was gone. Burned to the ground, side shed and all. Here and there an ember flickered and crackled and smoke rose into the evening sky but the building was no more.

In the distance he could see that the other cabins, scattered through the clearing, had been burned as well. Dreading what he might find, he forced himself to search the ashes, looking for the slightest indication of . . . bodies.

He could not bring himself to think about what he was really looking for: his parents. His brain would not allow it, though he knew the death smell came from someone. He could not allow himself to believe it was from them, from Mother and Father.

He found nothing in the ashes. And when he spread the search out around the cabin, moving in greater circles, he still found no trace that might have been his parents.

But as the search loop widened, he began to come across bodies—his neighbors, shot down and hacked where they'd fallen. They did not look like they had been people. What he found seemed more like trash, paper and cloth blown across the ground. But they were people, friends and families he had known. A frantic need took him, the thought that the next body might be the one he dreaded most to find, and he ran from one to another trying to identify them in the failing light. Most had been mutilated so badly it was hard to tell who they had once been.

Overton lay by his cabin, his shirtsleeves still not down on his wrists, chest and stomach filled with arrows, his scalp gone so his face drooped without the top-skin to hold it up.

Samuel ran from body to body in the gathering twilight until at last there were no more bodies to find. No matter how fast he ran, how wide he ran, he did not find his parents. Along with six or seven others, they had not been killed, or at least not been killed here. They had been taken away. They had not been killed. He clung to that thought—they had not been killed.

He stood, his breathing ragged, sobbing softly. Twice he had thrown up, and the smell and taste mixed with the tears of frustration and grief for his friends, and rage for what had been done to them. He knew that if he lived to be a hundred, he would never lose the taste, the smell or the images of what he had seen: the madness of what men could do to other men in savage rage.

Dark caught him now. He had circled through the settlement and was back at his own cabin, or where it had been. There was nothing left that would furnish light; all of the candles had melted. But he trapped some of the embers that were still glowing and made a campfire off from the cabin a bit. In its light he found the woodpile, which, oddly, had not been burned, and at the side of the pile there was a stack of pine-pitch knots and roots that his mother had used to start fires. The pitch concentrated in the knots burned with a smoky hot flame that lasted for an hour or more and would work as a torch. Near the garden plot he found the oak shovel they had used to turn the earth for gardening. The attackers had overlooked it or left it as useless, because anything of value had been taken or destroyed.

There were nine bodies to be buried before the coyotes, wolves and bear came. He knew that he would be moving come daylight, tracking, looking for sign, so the burying had to be done tonight.

Carrying spare pine knots and the shovel, he went from body to body. He dug a shallow grave next to each one, knowing that it might not be enough to protect them, that scavengers might dig them up, but so pressed for time that he had no choice. He covered each as best he could. Three were children and did not take as long, and though it was hard to tell exactly who they were in the dark and with the condition of the bodies, he remembered the children laughing and playing in front of the Olafsens' cabin, two boys and a little girl with a crude doll. He found the doll in the grass and wept as he buried it with the smallest body. He cried over each corpse, thinking of them living, thinking of them meeting in the cabin and living and talking and laughing and . . . just *being.* And now all gone. Gone. He could not stop crying, thinking of his parents, wondering, worrying.

It took five hours to bury everyone. It was still dark when he finished and looked around him. Then he realized that he should have said something over the bodies.

He did not know the right words—something about ashes and dust—but he took another torch and went back to each grave and bowed his head and said:

"Please, Lord, take them with you. Please."

It was all he could think to say and he hoped it was enough.

He went back to the campfire by his own cabin site and sat looking into the flames.

Praying.

Praying for safety for his parents.

And the others who had not been killed.

Praying for all who survived but praying most for his parents and, squatting there by the fire, also praying for daylight to come so he could begin looking for them.

And in half an hour, a little more, his eyes closed and sleep came and took him down, down, until he was lying on his side by the fire, sleeping deeply with all the bad dreams that he'd known would come; sleeping with twitches and jerks and whimpers at first, and then just sleeping.

Sleep.

The Americans

The American army consisted of three parts: the Continental (or regular) Army, the volunteer militia (including the elite Minutemen) and the Rangers, or small groups that were trained in guerrilla tactics.

The Continentals bore the brunt of the fighting and they were equipped much like the British, with smoothbore Brown Bess muskets and sometimes bayonets. Many of them also carried tomahawks, or small hand axes, which could be very effective once past the first line, the line of bayonets.

The militia volunteers were usually used to supplement the Continentals, but were quite often not as dependable or steady as they could have been had they been trained better, and they often evaporated after receiving the first volley and before the bayonets came. Most of them were also issued smoothbore muskets and some had bayonets for them, but others had rifles, which were very effective at long range but could not mount bayonets.

Special Ranger groups, such as Morgan's

Rifles, had an effect far past their numbers because of the rifles they carried. A rifle, by definition, has a series of spiral grooves down the inside of the barrel—with the low pressure of black powder, the rifling then was with a slow twist, grooved with a turn of about one rotation for thirty-five or forty inches. A patched ball was gripped tightly in the bore and the grooved rifling, and the long bore (up to forty inches) enabled a larger powder charge, which allowed the ball to achieve a much higher velocity, more than twice that of the smoothbores. And the high rate of rotation, or spin, stabilized the ball flight, resulting in greater accuracy.

CHAPTER 5

Samuel was just thirteen, but he lived on a frontier where even when things were normal, someone his age was thirteen going on thirty. Childhood ended when it was possible to help with chores; for a healthy boy or girl, it ended at eight or nine, possibly ten.

Because of his parents' nature—their lack of physical skills, their joy in gentleness, their love of books and music, their almost childlike wonder in *knowing* all they could about the whole wide world, but not necessarily the world right around them—Samuel had become the provider for his family.

As he embraced the forest, his skill at hunting grew. Actually, the forest embraced him, took him in, made him, as the French said, a *courier du bois,* a woods runner. Soon he provided meat for nearly the whole settlement, and in turn, the other men and women helped Samuel's parents with their small farm and took over Samuel's chores when he was in the woods.

Samuel's knowledge grew until when he heard a twig break, he would *know* whether it was a deer or bear or squirrel that broke it. He could look at a track and *know* when the animal or man made it, and whether or not the creature was in a hurry and if so, why, and how fast it was going and what, if anything, was chasing it and how close the pursuer might be.

And the more he was of the woods, of the wild, of the green, the less he was of the people. He sometimes enjoyed being with others, and of course he loved his parents. But his skills and his woods knowledge set him apart, made him different. His neighbors in the settlement saw this and they sought him out when they had a question about the forest or about game. They marveled at him, thought of him as a kind of seer, one who could know more than others, divine things in a spiritual way. Samuel knew this was not the case. He had just learned to see what others could not.

Now he brought to the fore all his knowledge to read sign as he met the day.

He was on his feet before the first light broke through the trees. He woke desperately thirsty and went to the creek that trickled past the rear of the cabin, and he drank long and hard. The water was so cold it hurt his teeth and so sweet it took some of the taste-stink from the evening before out of his mouth. He was hungry, but he could find no food that the marauders had overlooked. He would have to shoot something along the way.

For now, there was nothing to do but read sign and try to figure out what had happened, how it had happened and exactly when.

He started by circling the cabin, forcing himself to take time to be calm, carefully studying the ground, looking closely at the soft dirt away from the grass.

First he found small tracks from moccasins he had made for his mother. Then he saw his father's prints, also from moccasins, the right foot toed in slightly from a time when, showing off as a small boy, he'd broken his ankle jumping from a shed roof.

Both sets of prints were in the soft dirt in front of the door of the cabin, in the normal patterns they would make going in and out.

Then, in the dirt at the side of the cabin, more moccasin prints. Larger, flatter feet, digging deeper, running, as the attackers came. And still more prints, too many to tell them apart. On top of those, which meant they had come later, hard shoes with leather soles and heels. At least three men with regular shoes—two of normal weight and one heavier. On top of all the marks, Samuel saw horse prints. Two, maybe three horses, all unshod and being led, because there was no extra weight on them.

No men in the settlement wore shoes, or could afford horses to ride. Only one man had a single workhorse. Others who could afford animals had oxen, because when they became too old or broken to work, they could be eaten.

The attack had been fast. They had come up along the creek—Samuel backtracked and found their prints in the soft soil there—and exploded out in the clearing by the cabin. His parents were probably outside and must have been overrun with no time to react. His father wouldn't have had his musket close anyway. It was like him to leave it inside when working near the house.

Samuel's father had seen bad things happen to other people, but was too good inside, too generous, to believe that they could happen to him.

He must believe now, Samuel thought.

The attack widened rapidly. He saw where Overton and others had fallen, saw the blood, now covered with flies, where they had been hacked to the ground with tomahawks. It was a mystery to Samuel, though, why his parents had not been killed. He was grateful, but it didn't make any sense.

He lost their tracks as he followed the spreading attack. Larger moccasin prints and the shoe prints of the three men were everywhere. He could imagine the terror of the people in the settlement—the war cries of the attackers mixed with the screams of the victims and the smell of blood and fear and death.

He saw where at least two of the men in shoes had mounted their horses. Here and there he found single or double tracks of his mother and father as they were jerked or pulled—the tracks scuffed and misshapen. New tracks joined theirs as other people were also spared, all of them dragged or pushed toward the eastern side of the settlement.

Finally he saw how it had ended. The last of the cabins were burned, the surviving victims—probably neck-tied to each other with rope—lined up and pulled along the trail. The horses were in front and the attackers split, some in front and some in back. There was no indication that any prisoners had been wounded or killed.

When?

When had it happened?

He started following the tracks—which a blind man could have followed—and let his mind work on that question.

He'd left home early the day before, moving west until he came to new country, since he'd hunted out the forest around the settlement.

Say by midmorning he was out of earshot of gunfire—*if* anybody had used a gun. All the victims he'd buried had been chopped down with either tomahawks or war clubs.

So . . . the attack could have come midmorning. That would have been the soonest. If that was the case then they were just under twenty-four hours ahead of him. Maybe twenty, twenty-two. Moving slowly—as they would with prisoners—they might make two miles an hour. With a rest of perhaps six hours they might have traveled fourteen to sixteen hours. Twenty-four to twenty-eight miles.

He shook his head. Probably less. He studied the trail ahead and the spacing of the footprints, trying to estimate their speed. They were close together. Even the horses' tracks showed they were moving slowly. Twenty miles, at the most, yet still only a guess.

But he turned out to be wrong.

Later he discovered that he'd forgotten that there was another settlement of four cabins ten miles farther on.

And the attackers had taken the time to stop and slaughter the people who lived there.

The British

Generally poorly trained, the British enlisted soldier was also poorly paid—often going months with no pay at all—poorly cared for (the wounded were virtually ignored and allowed to die alone, unless a friend had time to help), poorly fed (salt beef, dried peas and tea were mainstays) and poorly treated (tied to a wagon wheel and flogged until his back was shredded for the slightest infraction).

And yet somehow, amazingly, up until the War for Independence he managed to conquer most of the world.

Young British officers in England, when they were being shipped out to fight in the colonies, were told to "settle your affairs and make out a proper will because the riflemen will almost certainly kill you."

CHAPTER 6

As he walked, Samuel felt as if he were following some kind of a killing storm.

Even the tracks seemed savage. From the footprints, it was evident that the prisoners, tied together, were constantly jerked and pulled to increase their speed. Their prints were scuffed, ragged, and he felt his mother's anguish terribly. She was small, and thin, and very strong in her own way, but this brutal treatment, probably with a rope around her neck, might be too much for her. If she was too slow they might . . . He could not finish the thought.

The shock Samuel had felt since he'd come upon the devastation in the settlement and dealt with the bodies had left him numb. Now it turned to anger, coming into rage, and that was worse because he had to remain calm.

He had no idea what to do except to follow his parents'

tracks—he saw their footprints now and then. He had to follow and rescue them. How he could do that, free his parents . . . he'd have to wait and see. Wait until he knew more.

He would learn by studying sign. He could not forget himself and his skills now. The people who were leaving the tracks were the people he had to deal with. He had to understand them by the time he caught up with them.

He stopped and tried to slow his harsh breathing, tried to still his mind and remember all he had taught himself about studying trails and the surrounding ground.

It seemed that all of the captors and captives were walking on the trail, but there might be others off to the side.

Quickly, he started to swing to the left and right of the trail. It was mostly grass, and hard to read, but at last he saw scuff marks and some moccasin tracks in open dirt. They had scouts on each side of the main group.

On the second swing, he found the first body. It was a man in his thirties who'd been picking berries when they'd come upon him. He must have had a rifle or musket—no one would be out in the woods without some kind of weapon—but it was gone, along with his powder horn and "possibles" bag. He had been scalped. Mutilated. Sadly, there was no time for Samuel to give him a decent grave. He scraped a slight trench with his knife and covered the body with a minimum of dirt. He bowed his head, then went back to the trail.

Covering the body hadn't taken much time, but it upset him. As he walked on, he tried to still the shaking of his hands. He picked up his speed, and came into the clearing of the next settlement before he was ready for it.

He thought he knew what he would find. It was just the few cabins, but unlike Samuel's home it had a name—Draper's Crossing.

And it was gone. At first it seemed the same devastation he had found at home. Smoke rising from burned cabins and sheds. But when he stopped, he saw that he wasn't alone.

On the southern side of the clearing, there was a figure. It was an old man. As Samuel approached, he saw that the man was spading dirt with a wooden shovel onto a mound that was clearly a grave.

And he was singing.

"Rock of ages,
cleft for me,
let me hide
myself in thee. . . ."

Samuel stopped ten yards away. He saw no weapon but he stood ready, rifle held across his chest, thumb on the hammer. As the old man patted the dirt with the shovel, Samuel could see four other grave mounds where the cabins had been. The man said in a singsong voice: "There to sleepy, little darling, there to sleepy with the

Jesus boy, all to sleepy, little darling, all to sleepy with the Jesus boy. . . ."

Samuel coughed, but the old man did not turn.

". . . Jesus came, the Jesus boy came and took them all up to heaven—"

"How long ago were they here?" Samuel finally interrupted the man's song.

The man turned toward Samuel and kept up his singing.

". . . Lordy, then the Jesus boy came and took them all to heaven. There was Draper and Molly and they came in and took them all to the Jesus boy. . . ."

"How long ago? Can you tell me when they were here?"

". . . in the dark they came. Took them all to the Jesus boy, took them all but not Old Bobby, no sir, didn't take Old Bobby 'cause Old Bobby he sat eating dirt and pointing up at the Jesus boy and talking through his ear holes, ear holes, and they thinking Old Bobby was teched but it wasn't so, wasn't so, wasn't so. . . ."

"Water. Is there water or food here?"

". . . wasn't teched at all, just knew how the Jesus boy could save us, save us, so I sat there eating dirt and laughing and praying. . . ."

With piercing, intense and otherworldly green eyes, he stared, but not at Samuel. He looked through Samuel at some far place that only he could see, only he could know. He picked up the shovel and started walking off to the south where Samuel could see one more burned cabin. Beside it lay what looked like a pile of rags, but Samuel knew it wasn't.

One more body . . .

Now he remembered something he had heard about the Indians. Considering that he had lived his whole life on the frontier, he knew very little about them, and what he did know he had learned by listening to adults, to rumors and stories they sometimes told after they'd had a little too much hard cider or blackstrap rum.

He remembered that some tribes saw crazy people as graced by the Higher Power, and that they believed that old people who did not think straight should be protected, or at least not harmed.

Which must be why they had let Old Bobby go.

"Maybe he is crazy," Samuel said aloud, watching him walk away with the shovel. "And maybe not . . . Either way, he's alive."

He turned back to the trail. If Old Bobby was right, they had come "in the dark." Probably just before dawn, if they had stopped to rest at all.

That meant Samuel was gaining.

And *that* meant he had to keep moving.

The World

The War for Independence very rapidly turned into something like a world war. Native Americans fought on both sides, and Spain got involved on the American side, or at least its navy did. Germany sent the mercenaries known as Hessians. The French were a staunch ally of the United States, with their navy keeping England from resupplying her troops and distracting it from the American navy. The English navy, in fact, was so preoccupied with the French that it could not focus on the American problem.

CHAPTER 7

He had been running for forty hours now. Just as he left Draper's Crossing, he passed a cornfield that the attackers had tried to burn. Some ears of corn had been roasted.

Hunger took him like a wolf and he grabbed a half-dozen ears, jamming them in his clothing. He ate as he walked, letting the sweet corn juice slide down his throat and into his stomach. The hunger was so intense that eating the corn made his jaws ache. The food made his body demand water. He hadn't taken time to find a well or where one was. When he came to a small creek, he stopped to drink.

The water was muddy where the creek crossed the trail, so he moved off into the thick underbrush twenty yards upstream to where the creek ran clear. He knelt to put his mouth to the water and this act saved his life.

His lips had no sooner touched the water than he heard men's voices. It was a native tongue and they were loud, and laughing. There were two of them. Had they come upon Samuel, they surely would have taken or killed him.

Samuel kept his head near the ground. Through small holes in the brush he could see them from the waist down. They wore leather leggings and high moccasins and each carried a musket in one hand—he could see the butts hanging down at their sides—and either a coupstick or a killing lance in the other. Both of the men had fresh scalps hanging on the shafts they carried.

For the first time in his life Samuel wanted to kill a man.

The overwhelming rage that he had begun to feel while following his mother's small footprints as she'd been savagely jerked along the trail was like a hot knife in his brain.

If there had only been one, he would have done it. But he carried no tomahawk. All he had was a skinning knife, and his rifle fired only one shot. After that, the one he didn't shoot would turn on him before he could reload. With only a knife to defend himself, he'd have almost no chance.

So he waited until they were out of sight; then, staying low and moving slowly, he went back to the trail.

Why had the men come back? Whatever the reason, two men alone would not backtrack too far into potentially hostile country. If there were any kind of force after them, they would want to keep moving.

So, Samuel thought—maybe I'm getting close.

He picked up the pace to a jog, but stayed well to the side of the trail on the edge of the thicker undergrowth in case he ran into any others. And again, this move saved his life.

Clearings left by old beaver ponds were scattered through the forest. Some were small, an acre or two; others were thirty or forty acres.

A large clearing popped up in front of Samuel now. It was late afternoon, almost evening, and the sun slanted from the west behind him into the clearing.

It was another stroke of luck. The clearing had been turned into a large encampment, filled with Indians, some British soldiers in red uniforms and, nearly a quarter of a mile away, freight wagons hooked up to horses.

Samuel slid into the underbrush. He crawled farther back where he couldn't be seen. Unfortunately he couldn't see, either, and he squatted in the thick foliage and tried to remember what he'd seen.

Three wagons ready to go out. Ten or fifteen soldiers, including three officers on horses, and ten or fifteen Indians.

He shook his head. No. Not so many soldiers. Seven or eight. And fewer Indians. Eight or nine.

One large fire in the center of the clearing, one smaller one closer to the wagons. A group of people huddled there.

The captives.

There hadn't been time to see them clearly and they were too far away for him to see if his mother and father were in the group.

In a rope pen near the wagons were one or two horses, three or four oxen, maybe a milk cow; there was also a spit set up over the larger fire with some kind of big animal cooking.

Which meant they were going to be here for some time, perhaps the night.

He settled slowly back on his haunches, careful not to move the brush around him.

He had caught up to them.

There was a chance his mother and father were with that group of captives. He still had no plan to rescue them. Everything he'd done was just to catch up, see if they were still alive. Could they be here? He hadn't come across their bodies on the trail, and there *were* captives by the fire. For the moment, that was enough.

The plan would come later.

It would be dark soon; there was still no moon. Now he was astonished that it had only been forty or so hours since he'd returned from the hunt. His whole life, everything in it and around it, was different now, torn and gutted and forever changed from all that it had been, and it would never be the same.

It would be dark soon.

And in the dark, he thought, with no moon, in the near pitch-dark of starlight, there might be possibilities.

He had no plan.

But it would be dark soon.

And just then, as he settled back to wait and think on some way to get to the captives without being discovered—the whole world blew up.

Warfare

The British procedure when fighting was to march at the foe in a close line, with two or three ranks of men. The front rank would fire at fifty or sixty yards, then drop back and reload while the second rank stepped forward and fired, dropping back and reloading while the back rank came forward and fired.

This "rolling volley" had the effect of creating a kind of mass firepower. The weapons were very simple, but it was almost impossible to stand against the line when the men grew close, quit firing altogether and charged, screaming. It took a special kind of courage to stand ready when a line of howling men ran at you with bayonets aimed at your stomach. Many times, American soldiers turned and ran rather than face what the British army called the Wall of British Steel.

CHAPTER 8

The natives began whooping and dancing around the large campfire, firing their muskets in the air in celebration.

Samuel crept out, slowly, until he could partially see what was going on. He started to move back under cover when there was a sudden increase in the racket. And the sound was different.

The Indians had been firing in the air as they danced, which caused the explosions to go up and away. They were firing smoothbore muskets, weapons that made a muffled barking sound. But this new sound had the sharper, cracking quality of higher-velocity rifles.

Samuel crept back out to the edge and saw that the shots had come from the north side of the clearing, where another trail came in.

Six or eight shots. Great clouds of black-powder smoke

came rolling out of the forest. A pause to reload, then eight more shots.

The Indians and British soldiers were stunned. A few Indians and one soldier went down, probably dead. Several others were wounded and hobbled into the brush for cover.

But the Indians and British recovered and returned fire. Samuel was jarred by two important facts: First, whoever was attacking, this might end in the rescue of his parents. Second, he should help them.

He moved to the clearing near the trail, raised his rifle, cocked it and, without thinking of the enormity of what he was doing, aimed at the nearest British soldier. He was less than fifty yards away. The German silver of Samuel's front sight settled on the red uniform. He set the first trigger and was moving his finger to the hair trigger when he heard a noise behind him.

He wheeled, his rifle coming around in time for him to see the two Indians who had nearly caught him earlier, running straight at him.

"Wha—" Half a word, then one Indian, the one farther away, leveled his musket and fired. Samuel felt the ball graze his cheek. Without thinking, his rifle at his hip, he touched the hair trigger and, in slow motion, felt the rifle buck, saw the small hole appear in the Indian's chest. Then, through a cloud of smoke from his weapon, he watched the Indian fall as he saw the other Indian swing a tomahawk in a wide arc. He knew he couldn't raise his rifle in time to block the blow. The tomahawk was coming at his head and he tried to duck, but the white-hot pain exploded as the side of the tomahawk smashed into his forehead.

And then, nothing.

Wounds

Untreated battle injuries often led to gangrene, which causes the body to literally rot away, turning first green, then black, from infection that travels rapidly. Because antibiotics were unavailable in the eighteenth century, amputation was the usual treatment. Due to the horrific odor of gangrene, surgeons could smell the patient and make an accurate diagnosis.

If the patient was not lucky enough to benefit from amputation, maggots would be introduced into the wound in an attempt to aid healing. They would eat away the infection.

Barring the surgical removal of body parts or the use of parasites, doing absolutely nothing and letting the patient die was the only option at the time.

CHAPTER 9

Strange dreams.

Visions of unreality.

Endless screams that started with low grunts and became more and more shrill until they cut his soul . . .

Dreams of his mother, dressed all in buckskins, ladling some kind of thick stew with a wooden spoon into a wooden bowl, chewing tobacco and spitting off to the side while she held the bowl out, shaking her head.

"He ain't anywhere near right yet." She spit her wad of tobacco juice out again. "Brains scrambled to hell and gone . . ."

Then a trapdoor came down, a lid, something thick and dark, and there was no light at all, just blessed darkness and sleep, sleep, sleep . . . and more screams.

No sense of time. Once he tried to remember his name

and fought with it for a minute or a day or a week or ten years. He couldn't tell.

More dreams. Scattered. His mother, this time wrapped in a blanket with stringy black hair hanging down at the sides of her head while she chewed an obnoxious cud. She disgorged it, slapped it on his head and tied it on with a filthy rag, spitting more tobacco juice out and nodding. "Got to get the pizen out or she's going to rot on him."

It was as if his eyes never really opened, as if he saw everything through closed lids, and the images that swirled through his mind were so mixed that they became a blur.

Night, day, night, day—light and darkness seemed to flop and flow over each other. Pictures would stick for a moment and then go.

A horse, then a cow, then his mother leaning down, still in the dirty blanket, greasy black hair hanging down the sides of her head, raising the poultice and grinning, spitting more tobacco juice. "Coming clean now," she said, "clear pus, looks clean as springwater, all the yeller gone."

And then bouncing, incredibly rough bouncing, as if someone were jumping on a bed while he was trying to sleep. He would pass out in pain, rolling waves of pain.

Finally a picture stopped, just stopped in front of his eyes, in front of his mind. Locked in.

It was dark, or night, and he was on some kind of wooden frame lying on the ground. A fire burned nearby and when he opened his eyes wide, the light from the fire seemed to shove a lance into the middle of his head. He grunted in pain. He closed his eyes and waited for the rolling pictures to begin again. When they didn't, he opened his eyes, but only in a slit.

The image was the same. A bed frame of some kind, a fire, and this time, less pain from the light. As he watched, an arm came out of nowhere and put a piece of wood on the fire, then withdrew.

He tried to move his head and see where the arm went but the pain was so intense he nearly lost consciousness. He lay back and closed his eyes, opened them again when the pain receded.

"Where . . . who . . . ?" The words pealed in his mind like a bell, echoing around inside his head.

A figure appeared next to the fire. Not his mother but a young man with stringy black hair and a cheek full of tobacco juice. He leaned down, his face close to Samuel's. "You in there righteous or are you going away again?"

"I'm . . . I'm here. Who are you?"

"John. John Cooper, but most just call me Coop."

"Where . . . ?"

"Long story, that. We be about twelve miles from where you got that egg on your head. Twelve miles in distance, more'n that in time."

"When . . . I don't remember . . . Some Indians. I think I shot at one and then . . . nothing. Why did I shoot at an Indian?"

"Cain't tell. We come on these Iroquois and some

redcoats. We'd already seen what they took and done back at Miller's Crossing, so we snuck up proper and took them on."

"I remember. You were shooting. You say 'we,' where are the others?"

"Asleep. I'm the night watch tonight, plus I've been doctoring you and I thought you might lose your light during the night. You been breathing like an old pump. I guess you was just sucking air hard because you didn't die. Course it could still happen. I had a cousin got kicked in the head by a mule—they's fractious, mules—and he lived for nigh on two months 'fore he lost his light. He never talked none except now and again a kind of moan—like somebody stepping on a duck. Then he just up and died."

Samuel closed his eyes, felt a spinning. Then, as if a fog were lifted, it all came back.

"I was tracking Ma and Pa. They . . . I mean the red-coats, the Indians . . . hit our place while I was looking for bear. They killed most everybody but took my parents and a few others captive."

Coop nodded. "We saw them, all around a fire. Ropes tyin' 'em together."

"What happened to them?"

Coop shrugged. "Wasn't much of a fight. We fired once, reloaded, laid out another round, and they ran. Them redcoats had wagons already hooked up and they piled the captives in the wagons and lit out. We couldn't shoot no more for fear of hitting the captives. The Indians just drifted away, like smoke. That would have been that except one of them put a musket ball in Paul. It was in his gut—awful place, that. We knew he was going to die—ain't nobody comes back from a belly wound—and kept waiting for it, but he made four days. He gave up his light last night. No, night before. Died screaming. It was bad. Surprised it didn't bring you out of your stupor, the screaming. Kept everybody up all night."

Samuel closed his eyes again, trying to put numbers together. Died one, two days ago, after making four days; if a belly wound took four days to kill and it happened the day of the fight but Paul died two days ago . . . "How long since they took the captives? Since the fight?"

"Five, six days. You been out six days. We like to not found you and when we did, we almost left you. Thought you was with the raiders."

"Me? Why?"

"Well, you wasn't with us, so we thought you was with them. But Carl did some thinking on it—Carl's my brother and he's the one to think on things—and said look how messed up your head was where they clubbed you and look at the bullet hole in the Indian you killed—that's a honey of a little rifle you got—and how could you be with them and still get clubbed and shoot one of them, so we took you with us."

"I've been out six days?"

"Closer to seven, counting the night."

"And did you say we'd come twelve miles?"

Coop nodded. "First three days—no, four—we let you to lay. Everybody thought you would die and there wasn't no sense dragging you. Then there was Paul, with his belly wound. If we tried to move him he would scream like a panther. Then we rigged up a drag and started to pull you back of one of them oxen they left behind when they ran."

"All the bumping."

Coop nodded, spit tobacco juice in the fire and listened to it hiss. "We couldn't stay too long and thought you could die just as well dragging as you could laying up somewhere. If we'd left you, something would have come along and ate you, so . . . here you are."

"My head . . ."

Coop nodded. "Good cut from that 'hawk. Carl took some deer sinew he had and an old needle he carries for fixings and sewed it up right pert'. He said in case you lived wouldn't be much of a scar. Across your forehead." Coop smiled and with some pride added, "It come on to having green pus and everybody knows that's bad, so I made up a spit and 'baccy poultice and tied it on with a piece of rag. Pus cleared up in two days."

"So I've been laying for six days?"

Another nod. "Coming on seven."

"Well, how . . ." With a start, Samuel realized he didn't have any pants on underneath the coarse blanket that covered him. "How come I'm not all messed up?"

"We took your pants off. Got them wrapped in a blanket pack with your rifle. Indian must have been in a hurry or he would have took it, sweet little shooter like that. Also got your possibles bag and powder horn. What you feel under your rear is fresh grass. Anytime you messed we just threw the old grass away and pulled in a half a foot of fresh new grass. Slick as a new calf, or maybe slick as a baby's bottom."

"Maybe I should put my leggings on."

"Only if you ain't going out of your head again."

"I don't think so."

"Suits me. I was the one having to get new grass all the time. You ain't et nothing other than a little broth I got down you one time and some water now and again. Man can go long time without food, no time at all without he has some water."

"I'm starving," Samuel said automatically, but with the words came the feeling and he realized he was as hungry as he'd ever been.

"You'd ought to drink something soft first." Coop handed him a wooden bowl with a mixture of broth and meat. "Go slow. This is from some salted ox they was cooking when we jumped them."

Samuel took the bowl. He tried to drink slowly, but as the taste and smell hit him he couldn't help gulping at it, meat and all, so fast that he gagged and threw up.

"Slow," Coop repeated, coming back with a blanket roll and putting it on the ground next to Samuel. "You'll founder, you don't go slow."

Samuel started over carefully. There was silence as he

ate, chewing completely before swallowing, small bites, small swallows.

It's like fire, he thought, when you're cold. Fire moving through your body. He ate the first bowl, handed it to Coop and watched him refill it, this time with broth and chunks of glistening fat as well as meat.

This second bowl he drank and ate more slowly than the first, and while he ate he made a mental list of questions to ask when his stomach was full.

Why are you here? How many of you are there? Where are you going? Is there any way you can help me find my mother and father? Are you, will you, can you, do you . . . questions roaring through his mind.

He finished eating.

He lay back.

He opened his mouth to ask the first question and his eyes closed at the same instant and he was immediately asleep.

And the last thing he thought as he went under was that he still hadn't put his pants on.

American Spirit

Although poorly trained and weakly led and improperly fed—so badly that soldiers sometimes had to eat their shoes—the Americans took comfort from fighting on home soil and usually had much higher morale than the British. While they were often outnumbered and fought with inferior equipment, this spirit had an enormous effect and they took the phrase "morale is to fighting as four is to one" to heart on the battlefields.

CHAPTER 10

This time the sounds of men coughing and axes chopping wood for the fire awakened Samuel. He opened his eyes—the pain was much less—and saw that it was daybreak. Men were moving all around him.

He started to roll, but the head pain stopped him, as well as the sudden memory that he had no pants on. The bedroll was next to him where Coop had put it. He snaked his pants out, pulled them on and fastened them with the leather cord around the waist.

The pain in his head had abated; it only jabbed if he moved suddenly. The wound felt tight, as if someone were pulling the top of his scalp together.

When he unrolled the blanket, his rifle half fell out and he saw that the lock had dirt jammed around the flint and pan, pushing up the striker plate, or frizzen, so the rifle was not able to fire.

The men were making fire, tying bedrolls. One man had what looked to be a permanently bent left arm held up at a slight angle. He was sitting on the ground cleaning his rifle. It made Samuel feel embarrassed that his own lock was so dirty. He found his possibles bag in the blanket roll. This was a pouch with the powder horn attached that hung around his neck, where he carried odds and ends of equipment for cleaning and firing his rifle. Inside, he had a tiny piece of steel wire. After blowing the dirt out of the pan and frizzen and flint, he used the wire to clear the touch hole, which fed the jet of flame from the pan into the powder charge. Then he used an oily rag to clean the whole area and put some finely ground black powder into the pan. This was the ignition powder that the flint-metal sparks would fire into the powder charge. He closed the frizzen over the pan, eased the hammer to half cock, safety, and set the rifle aside.

The fire had flared up as the men added wood. Samuel rose to his feet and went into the nearby bushes to relieve himself. His legs were wobbly but seemed to work well enough, even though he felt weak as a kitten. As one part of his body got better, another would follow. As the pain in his head went down, the hunger in his belly came up.

There was the entire back leg from an ox over the fire on a metal spit. Last night Coop had been cutting bits of it to put in Samuel's broth. Looking at it made Samuel even more ravenous.

But the other men weren't eating, so he held back. One, a thin man with a scraggly beard, saw Samuel looking at the meat. He pulled a knife, really a short sword, carved off a generous piece and handed it to Samuel.

"You got to eat. We might walk long today and it's going to be hard for you to keep up without your belly is full."

"Thank you." Samuel took the meat—it was very tough—and he sat chewing and swallowing, watching the men clear up camp.

While Samuel watched the men and ate, he also rolled and tied up his bedroll, making certain his powder was dry and his possibles bag was ready to go. But these men were even faster.

Without speaking except to grunt and point, they seemed to get everything done with the least effort and in the quickest time. The ox was yoked and tied off to a tree. The skid that Samuel had been on, which had two long tongues that went up either side of the ox and attached to the yoke, was hooked up and packed with extra equipment—the cooking pot, blankets, muskets, a small keg of powder and another of whiskey, and, of all things, a drum left by the fleeing redcoats and Indians.

Then the men came and stood by the fire. In silence, they cut pieces of meat and ate, drinking creek water out of a wooden bucket with a wooden dipper.

Samuel still had dozens of questions but since the men were silent as they stood staring into the fire while they chewed, he held his tongue.

There were seven men. When everybody was done

eating, they each took a plug of tobacco and poked it in their cheek or lower jaw. They put the leftover meat on the skid, wrapped in a piece of green ox hide to keep the flies off, then used the bucket to fetch water from the creek to put the fire out.

With no effort at all, they were moving along the trail.

Two men went well ahead, one left, one right of the trail. The rest formed a column—if five men could be called a column—just ahead of the ox and Samuel.

In Samuel's weakened condition, there was absolutely no way he could have kept up with the men.

But the ox saved him. He knew that oxen tend to plod a little less than two miles an hour, and this ox was slower yet. Even Samuel had no trouble keeping up with him, and when his legs felt a little weak, he would move to the ox's side and hold on to the yoke, letting the ox pull him along for a time.

Every hour and a half the two men walking ahead would come in and two others would move out. On one of these cycles, Coop came back and walked near Samuel.

It was what Samuel had been waiting for.

"You kept me alive. Thank you."

"It weren't much. A little tobacco and spit and tough meat."

"I'd have been done if you hadn't come along."

"Maybe. Maybe not. One never knows how a wind is going to blow."

"Why *did* you all come along? Where are you going?"

Coop spit—the men all spit, almost all the time. Samuel had once tried tobacco, first in a clay pipe, then taking a chew, and it had made him sick as a dog. He couldn't see the sense in using it, but all these men seemed to chew all the time. And spit like fountains. Maybe something happened to your taster when you got older, he thought, so you didn't mind it.

"We're going to jine up," Coop said, pointing east with his chin, "and fight them redcoats. There be a feller named Morgan roundabout Boston City starting up Morgan's Rifles. We all shoot rifles and we figure to give them redcoats a taste of good shooting. They got nothing but muskets, good for nothing after fifty, sixty yards. Carl here"—he pointed up to where his brother walked beside the head of the ox—"he can pink a man on a horse out to two, three hundred yards. Every time. Wouldn't even know what hit him, nor where it come from. . . ." He nodded his chin at the group. "Every man here can hit a foot-square piece of paper every time at two hundred yards. I s'pose you could, too, took a mind to it."

"I'm not sure about killing."

"You did that Indian back there. Laying dead and had a bullet hole in him."

"I wasn't aiming. He shot and I pulled the trigger."

"What you gonna do when you find your mam and pap? Shake hands with them that took 'em?"

Samuel felt like spitting, too. "I haven't thought that far yet."

"Best be thinkin' on it, and keep your powder dry and your pan primed."

"Right. Thing is, I didn't even know there was anybody to fight. Who was good or bad, which side to be on."

Coop snorted. "Don't take much thinkin'. Them that starts in to killing people for no reason, them that comes and takes your folks with a rope around their necks—they's the bad ones. Your good people don't do that."

"What reason—" Samuel stumbled on a rock. To his surprise, the ox was aware of it and hesitated to let him catch up. "Why did those British redcoats and Indians attack us like that? There was no reason. We weren't against the Crown or rebels or anything."

Coop spit, neatly taking a fly off the ox's ear. He snorted. "Redcoats doing it because they's redcoats and ain't worth a tinker's damn. Follerin' orders. Indians doing it because they was hired to do it. They's Iroquois, most of 'em work for the English, always have, always will. Ever since that French War. They get all the plunder they can carry and scalp money from the redcoats. Heard there's a man named Hamlin, some kind of redcoat officer, buys so many scalps they call him Hair Buyer Hamlin. What I don't understand is why they took your folks instead of killin' . . . Oh look, the front line is comin' in."

The column stopped by a clear-water creek and everybody drank. Then the men took the meat off the drag and sat in a circle cutting pieces and chewing. At first Samuel hung back but Carl motioned him to squat and eat.

Samuel was feeling stronger by the minute and the meat heated him like fire.

No one talked much except for Coop, and when they finished, they rose, took a chew of tobacco and set off. Coop and another man went ahead.

Samuel walked in silence, hanging on to the wooden shaft tied to the ox. It was midmorning and the sun fell through tall trees on either side of the trail so they seemed to be walking in a lighted green tunnel. Now and then insects caught sunlight and flashed white like small lamps. Any other time, Samuel would have been taken by the beauty of it.

But now he could not stop thinking of what Coop had started to say.

Why *hadn't* the raiders killed his parents? And would they do it now?

I'm way behind them, he thought, six, maybe seven days. Dragging along with an ox. God only knows what's happening to them.

I have to go faster.

The Hessians

The British also used mercenary soldiers, issued with the same Brown Bess musket and bayonet. Most of them were troops from Germany, called Hessians. While they were relatively effective as combat soldiers, they brought with them such savage, atrocious behavior, and committed war crimes so far outside civilized behavior—bayoneting unarmed captive soldiers who had surrendered, farmers, women (including pregnant women), children and even infants—that they became known as little more than beasts and were treated in kind.

CHAPTER 11

He lay under overhanging hazel brush and studied the farm—here, very close to the middle of the wild, was an almost perfect little farm.

It had been three days since Samuel left the men behind. He'd eaten more and more meat, become stronger and stronger, and, at last, couldn't stand the slowness of walking beside the ox. The men were in no particular hurry; or, as Coop said, "Still gonna be a war, catch it now or catch it later." And they had gear to move, so had to go slowly.

But Samuel became more frantic with every step. At last, when they'd stopped to rest, he had told Coop he was going to take off on his own.

Coop had nodded. "There'll be people wantin' to kill you," he said. "Well. Let me cut those stitches out of your head. Healed up good." He set to work as he spoke.

"Almost everybody you meet will maybe want to kill you, so keep to the brush, keep your head down and don't walk where others walk." He took out the last stitch.

There was nothing more to say, so, with a nod, Samuel turned away and trotted ahead of Coop and the rest of the men.

Samuel took the advice to heart and worked well off the trail, which was becoming more like a road with two tracks. Even so, he doubled his speed.

He had brought meat with him and took care to eat sparingly. After three days, it was nearly gone. He'd have to get more soon. Deer were as thick as fleas and it was just a matter of shooting one. He was moving quietly through the woods, ready to do just that, when he came upon the farm.

It had not been attacked and burned. It was a shock to see buildings standing and unharmed.

And aside from that, this was a proper farm, not a frontier cabin hacked out of the woods. True, there was deep forest all around it, but the farm itself was neat as a pin, with split-rail fences all whitewashed and a frame house, and a barn made not from logs but from milled lumber. More, the house was painted white and the barn red, with white trim on the doors and windows. As he watched, he could see chickens in the yard.

Several thoughts hit him.

First, chicken would taste good. The thought of a roasted chicken made him salivate.

Second, if they hadn't been attacked it must mean they were friendly to the raiders, who must have come right through here.

Third—an easy jump in thinking—it would be all right for Samuel to "confiscate" a chicken, assuming the farmer was friendly with Samuel's mortal enemy.

Now, how to bring it about?

He could wait until dark, but that was still at least eight hours away. He couldn't waste time sitting here.

The farm was in the middle of a large clearing.

The tree line came close to the barn. If he worked his way through the trees, he might get close enough to grab a chicken and run.

He was moving before he stopped thinking of it. Since he saw no people as he moved around to the clearing in back of the barn, he moved fast. He kept the barn between him and the house to block their view. In moments he stood against the barn wall not ten feet from a small flock of chickens pecking at the ground.

Just as he started to make his move, he heard a scraping sound overhead and a barn loft door opened. A little girl, eight or nine, was looking down at him.

"I saw you through a crack in the wall the whole way. You thought you was sneaking, but I saw you. You looked like a big, two-legged deer. What's wrong with your head? How come you're running like that? What are you after—oh, the chickens. You want a chicken, go ahead. I don't like them anyway."

Samuel was so stunned he couldn't say anything, then he croaked in a whisper: "Is there anybody else here?"

"They's all up the house eating. They's eating squash and it makes me puke, so I came to the loft to play with my dolls. Go ahead, I won't tell."

"Thank you."

"Take that big red one. She's mean. Chases me all *over* the yard and pecks at my toes."

In for a penny, in for a pound, Samuel thought. He made a darting motion and, by luck, actually caught the big red chicken. It squawked once but he held it tight and it quieted.

He started to leave, then turned. "What's your name?"

"Anne Marie Pennysworth Clark," she said, "but everybody calls me Annie."

"Well, thank you, Annie. I've got to be going now." He turned to leave, but her next words stopped him.

"You look just like the man who was here, 'cept he was older and his head wasn't all cut up."

"What man?"

"Some men and a woman came here, some on horses and some in a wagon."

At that instant an enormous man holding a rifle came around the end of the barn. He had shoulders like a bear and his gun was pointed at Samuel's face. Samuel dropped the chicken, raised his own rifle and aimed it at the center of the man.

After a second, Samuel lowered his weapon. As soon as

it moved, the man dropped his. Samuel had forgotten to breathe. He took a deep breath now.

"My name is Samuel," he said.

"I thought a fox was in the chickens when I heard the hen squawk." The man shrugged. "Wasn't too far off."

"I don't steal"—Samuel's face burned—"but I've been on some rough trail and I got hungry."

"He wasn't stealing, Pa," Annie piped up. "I told him to take that red one. She keeps trying to eat my toes."

"I never turned anybody away from my door hungry," the man said. He held out his hand. "Caleb Clark—come up to the house and eat."

It all seemed so natural and open that Samuel forgot his earlier suspicion that the farmer was on the enemy's side. He took the man's hand. "Thank you, sir."

"Let's stop by the pump and wash your head first. It's a sight. Ma will have a fit."

"I got hit by an Indian—and these men came along and sewed me up."

"It looks," Caleb said, smiling, "like you got hit by a club and then some men stitched it up and smeared some kind of dark mud or something on it."

"Tobacco juice," Samuel said. "And spit. They made a poultice. And it saved me."

They were at the watering trough and pump. Caleb took Samuel's rifle—Samuel handed it over without thinking. Caleb held Samuel's head under the pump and started working the handle.

"Scrub," he said, pumping harder.

Samuel winced at the pain, but went to work. Carefully.

Finally the wound was clean enough to suit Caleb and they went to the house. Annie followed and, sure enough, the red hen pecked at her toes. Annie yelped and scurried ahead of Samuel and Caleb to the house.

Samuel had never been in anything but a cabin, most often with a dirt floor or at best a crude plank one, and Caleb's house seemed too fine, as if Samuel somehow shouldn't be allowed in; at least not without being boiled clean first.

The house inside was as neat as the outside, with plastered white walls and a sugar-pine board floor, polished and rubbed with beeswax.

"Company, Ma," Caleb said. "You got another plate?"

Caleb's wife was quite round, with red cheeks and hair up in a bun. She had flour dust on her cheek. She pushed a bit of hair back and smiled at Samuel with the briefest of looks. She pointed at a chair that backed to the stove. "Sit and eat, we just started."

There were only three people, four with Samuel, but the table absolutely groaned with food. There was squash, as Annie had said, with maple sugar and butter melted in the middle. There was a roast of venison and potatoes, a loaf of bread with apple butter and some kind of jelly, and corn on the cob with melted butter dripping from the cobs.

Samuel had never seen anything like it. Huge bowls of food, and a gravy tub that held at least a quart of rich brown steaming-hot gravy. His stomach growled as Caleb poured him some buttermilk and they all sat. There were a fork and spoon and knife at each place. Samuel waited to see how things were done. Caleb smiled. "We'll say grace."

They held hands, which seemed strange. Annie was to his left—she decided that since he was there she'd sit to eat—and she grabbed his hand. Caleb's big paw took his other hand and in a deep voice he rumbled:

"Thank you, Lord, for this food and this company. In Jesus' name, amen."

And they set to. Nobody spoke. Ma heaped his plate with food. It seemed more than he could possibly eat—he was sure his stomach had shrunk—but he somehow got it all tucked in and felt full as a tick.

Then Ma brought out rhubarb pie with thick cream sprinkled with maple sugar and somehow he got *that* down as well.

"Thank you, ma'am," he said. "I've never eaten like that, not in my whole life. Even at fall feast it wasn't that good, or that much. I won't have to eat for a week. I just wish my folks . . ."

He stopped, remembering what Annie had said. He turned to her. "You said some men came and one of them looked like me."

Caleb cut in. "Some British soldiers came here with two wagons holding fugitives or captives. Five of them. I fed the soldiers and they were civil enough and didn't bother us, though I heard some bad stories of the Hessians that hit some farms east of here. Then I took food and water out to the captives and one man, had his wife with him, was very polite and thanked me. He looked like you, same eyes and nose."

"He was my father. And that was my mother."

Samuel looked down at the floor and blinked away the burning in his eyes. Annie softly patted his shoulder.

He told the story of the attack, leaving out the worst details because of Annie. When he was finished, Ma was crying and he was having trouble holding tears back himself.

"When were they here?" he asked. "How long ago?"

"Two, no, three days. After they ate, they watered the horses, and while they were waiting for the horses to blow and settle the water, the lead officer pulled out a little traveling chessboard. I don't know how to play but he went to the captives and your pa sat and played a game with him on the edge of the wagon."

"He loves chess."

"I heard the officer say to another soldier that the only reason he brought your father was that he saw a chessboard when they raided the cabin and he wanted somebody to play with."

Thank God, Samuel thought. Thank God for such a little thing to mean so much. His father's life spared for a chessboard. His mother's life, too. He stood. "Thank you for the food. I have to be going. If I'm only three days behind and they keep taking it slow, I could catch them."

Caleb said, "They're headed for New York. The city. The British hold it and they keep a lot of prisoners there in old warehouses and out in the harbor on old ships. If you don't catch them along the trail you might just go there. Good luck to you, son. We'll keep you in our prayers."

Ma pressed more food on him—venison, potatoes and corn, wrapped in a piece of linen. Annie and Ma hugged him and Caleb shook his hand. Then he trotted slowly, his stomach still heavy, out of the yard to the edge of the woods, where he entered thick forest.

He stayed well off to the side of the trail. Once again, this small act saved his life.

He heard one clink—metal on metal—and dropped to his stomach, out of sight, though he could see through gaps in the brush.

He watched them pass: an organized body of troops with tall hats moving at a quickstep in a tight formation. They followed an officer on a large bay horse. They did not look like British soldiers—they had brownish instead of red uniforms and were more disciplined than the redcoats. Hessians, he thought, Germans.

They were quickly past Samuel. Their march would take them directly to Caleb's farm. Curious, and with some fear, Samuel turned and followed them, off to the side, fifty yards to the rear.

He'd relive that decision for many sleepless nights.

The attack was over in minutes.

The Hessians quick-marched into the yard, broke formation and spread out into the farmyard, grabbing chickens as they moved.

Caleb and Ma came out onto the porch. Caleb wasn't armed, though he raised his arm and pointed at the soldiers.

He and Ma were immediately gunned down. Then four soldiers jumped to the porch and bayoneted them. Annie exploded out of the house and ran toward the barn. Three or four of the soldiers shot at her but missed, and once she was around the barn she ran for the trees. More men tried to hit her but missed. Samuel was amazed at how fast she ran. She stumbled once and it looked as if she might be hit, but she jumped to her feet and kept running.

They took the bodies of Caleb and Ma and dragged them back into the house. Eight or ten men went in the house then and looted it, taking anything shiny and all the food they could find.

Then they set fire to the house and barn and when those were roaring with flames, the soldiers fell into formation and quick-marched out of the yard, disappearing down the trail.

It had taken less than ten minutes.

Samuel was sickened by the cruelty, the absolute viciousness, of the attack, and he hunched over and retched. He felt that he should have run to Caleb and his wife, to help in some way, but knew there was nothing he could have done. He would have been dead long before he'd got at them.

He was helpless. He sat crying, watching the house and barn burn, the Hessians gone like a plague. Caleb and Ma. The food, eating together, how open and gentle and pleasant and good it had been to sit with them and talk.

Destroyed. Gone.

Gone in this ugly war with these evil men. Gone and never coming back and there was nothing, nothing, he could do or could have done to save them, help them.

Except find Annie.

Take her with him to New York.

He made certain nobody was coming down the trail, then set off at a trot around the clearing, staying well in the undergrowth, looking for Annie and trying to erase from his mind what he had seen.

He had to find Annie. Then find his parents.

That was all that mattered.

PART 3

GREEN
New York—1776

War Orphans

Children orphaned by war, as countless were during the Revolutionary War, suffer from nightmares and sleeping problems, headaches, stomachaches, anger, irritability and anxiety. Severely traumatized children may become withdrawn, appearing numb and unresponsive and sometimes becoming mute. When the danger and devastation end, children can show remarkable resilience and recovery if they are in a safe and stable environment where they are cared for and nurtured.

After the Revolutionary War, however, many orphans, if they were not taken in by other family members, grew up in institutions. Formal adoptions were very rare.

CHAPTER 12

He found Annie huddled in some hazel bushes, crying. When she saw him, she ran and threw herself at him, grabbing the edge of his shirt, silent except for the soft sobbing.

For three days.

Unless she was asleep or tending to herself, she would not get more than four feet away from him for three solid days. She held on to his clothing and did not say a word in all that time. At night he would wrap her in his blanket and sit away from the glow of the fire and doze, and she would cry in her sleep, almost all night.

It bothered him that she had no shoes or moccasins, and he had no leather to make a pair for her, but her bare feet were amazingly tough and she kept up with his rapid pace much better than he would have expected.

They drank from creeks, which were common, and

shared the small amount of food Ma had given him. Annie did not eat for the first three days and he worried at that—although she drank—but in the evening of the third day she took some food and seemed to come out of the cloud she was in, little by little.

He was having a very difficult time. With almost everything. The jolt from what his life had been just short weeks ago to what it was now had been so sudden, the gulf so vast, that he felt he was in a completely different world, one dominated by violence and insanity.

The woods were the one thing he knew and still believed in. He was thankful for the haven of the forest as they traveled.

Still, his rage would not go away. He stifled it, but he seethed with anger every time he thought of the Hessians and how they had killed the Clarks, of how they had tried to kill Annie, of how the raiders had slaughtered the peaceful settlers for no reason.

He wanted to punish them, make them pay for what they'd done, and could think of nothing to do except act as insane and violent as they had.

Kill someone.

Find someone in a red coat and shoot him.

He knew it was not something he could do, even though he thought of it. And so he drove himself—and, unfortunately, Annie—in a forced march that covered over fifteen miles a day. It would not have been so hard except that the trail had become a proper road. There was still forest on either side, but settlements, then small towns, appeared regularly. They often saw local people or detachments of redcoats marching on the road.

They avoided everybody. Samuel trusted no one, not even people who might have been friendly. Annie complained only once.

"We jump into the woods every time we see somebody," she said. "They can't all be bad."

"Yes," Samuel said, thinking of the Hessians, "they can. Every single one of them can be bad. So we hide. And that's it." His voice had an edge that kept her from arguing.

They worked around settlements and small towns, sticking to the trees, and on day five—they'd been out of food for a day and a half—Samuel shot a deer and took an afternoon, well back in the woods, to make a small fire with flint and steel and a little powder. He cooked the two back legs of the deer with stakes holding them over the fire and, when the meat was still rare, cut pieces from one of the legs, and they ate it squatting by the fire. He also cut off the strips of meat alongside the lower backbone—the tenderloin. Although it was quite small, he cooked that as well, to save for later.

They ate a whole back leg sitting there, until Annie's face was coated with grease. They wrapped the excess in the cloth Ma had given him and were up and moving again, Samuel not wanting to waste daylight.

He could think of little but finding his parents and

getting them away from their captors. But he also realized that the odds were not good. He knew nothing of cities, or even towns, but New York City must be large, and filled with people who would not be helpful since the British were there. Try as he might, he couldn't think of a way to get into the city safely to find his mother and father.

With meat in his belly he fairly loped along, so fast that at last Annie gasped, "You got to slow down. I can't run like a deer."

He slowed but kept the pace steady, so that when it was dark, hard dark, and he stopped, Annie fell asleep almost the instant he wrapped the bedroll blanket around her.

He decided to make a cold camp and didn't start a fire. Since there was no smoke, the bugs, mostly mosquitoes, found him at once. They weren't as bad as they'd been on his hunting trips on the frontier, but then he'd always had a fire with the smoke to keep them away.

He was tired, although not like Annie, and he had some thinking to do. It took him a while to get his mind off the mosquitoes, and by that time there was a new sliver of a moon. In the pale silver light he saw Annie's face, wrapped in the blanket, just showing enough to let her breathe, and his heart went out to her.

She was only eight, he thought, maybe nine, and her whole world had been absolutely destroyed.

Were there many like her? Everything gone because of this war? The innocent ones were the worst part of it all. His mother and father making a life on the frontier, just wanting to be left alone, his mother trying to get the garden to grow, his father learning how to use tools, how to make his own house, wanting only to work and read and think and live a quiet, simple life with his family.

All gone. His own life gutted, not as much as Annie's, but enough.

He had to get his parents back.

How? What to do? There were so many unknown factors that the questions seemed impossible.

He was one person with a rifle.

Oh yes, he thought, smiling grimly, and a knife.

And he felt that the entire world he was heading into was against him. He would have to get around them, the people in that world, some way, somehow. . . .

How?

His eyes closed, opened, closed again, his questions spiraling down as he leaned back against a tree and slept.

Civilian Deaths

Civilian mortalities have always been underreported in wars, and are nearly impossible to verify. Most historians and governments are forced to guess at the numbers because not only are birth and death certificates, church records, tax rolls and emigration documentation frequently destroyed during combat, but the true numbers are, in many cases, never counted, in order to hide them from a country's own people as well as the enemy.

Once mass weapons such as cannons and guns were developed and used by the military, far more civilians were killed simply by being in the wrong place at the wrong time.

CHAPTER 13

The signs were on the side of a tree, two boards hacked into the shape of an arrow and nailed up with large, handmade cut nails.

One pointed to a trail that went straight south. Crude letters: "Philadelphia—41 m."

The other arrow pointed straight east: "New York—38 m."

"What do they say?" Annie asked. "I can get the letters but I can't put them together so good. Yet."

Samuel told her. "About the same to either place. A three-day walk. . . . Let's get off the trail. I've got to think on it."

They moved back into the undergrowth and settled out of sight.

"What's to think about?" Annie said. "We go to New York to get our ma and pa."

She did not realize what she said, but Samuel heard the *our*. Something had happened in her mind, she'd found a way to stand it all, to keep going.

Samuel nodded.

What had Caleb said? Oh yes, New York was British.

But the Americans still held Philadelphia, the center of the new government. Had his mother and father come by here and seen this sign? Did they know that safety and refuge were just forty miles away, and then did they have to go on to New York?

He shook his head.

"I should . . . I ought to take you into Philadelphia, where it's safe, and find a place for you."

"No."

"But—"

"No. I ain't going to leave you. You're the only family I have. It won't help to leave me someplace because I'll just run and follow you. No matter what you say. We're going to find our folks. That's all there is to it. We're going to New York."

"What I was going to say—"

"Together."

"—was that it would take too long to go down there and come back—six or seven days—so I guess we'll stick together."

"Good. That's settled."

Samuel almost smiled. She looked so ragged—her dress was indescribably dirty and so was her face. Her hair stuck out at odd angles. The dirt was caked on her legs, and her feet looked like shoe leather—and yet she was ready to do what had to be done. I'm proud, he thought, to have you as a sister.

"All right then," he said. "Let's go."

They had a stroke of luck after they turned toward New York. Later that day they saw a farm with fresh corn in the field. They crept into the edge of the field and took enough ears for dinner.

Just after leaving the field, back in the woods alongside the trail, they heard an awful racket coming up the road from the rear. Something on wheels was clanging and clanking and rattling along. They were far enough back in the thickest part of the undergrowth so they couldn't see what it was. It stopped nearby.

All was quiet, and then Samuel heard dogs panting. Before he and Annie could move, two black-and-white mostly collie dogs came up to them in the brush, looked at them each for a moment—directly into their eyes—and gently tried to push them out toward the road, using their shoulders against Samuel's and Annie's legs.

"Hey!" Samuel whispered. "Leave off!"

He heard a laugh.

"You might as well come out of there," a coarse, deep voice shouted. "I know right where you are and I've got a two-gauge swivel gun aimed at you."

"You stay here," Samuel whispered to Annie. "I'll see what's going on."

But no, she was not going to stay, and they both stood and walked out of the brush, the collies nudging them along.

A huge freight wagon stood on the road, so stacked up with all sorts of everything—from bundles of rags to loops of tin pots tied up like garlands, to two saddles, to barrels and buckets and a rocking chair—that it looked enormous: a junk pile on wheels being pulled by two scruffy mules.

"How's your day?" the man on the wagon asked, spitting, and in such a thick Scottish brogue that it was difficult to understand him. "I'm Abner McDougal, tinker at large. The two dogs are William and Wallace—named after a Scottish hero." He saw Samuel's rifle and he held up his hands. "Don't shoot, I was making a jest about the swivel gun. I'm not armed, as you can see—don't believe in shooting things."

He seemed to be dressed in sewn-together rags and looked as untidy as the junk he was carrying. His voice had a horrible rasping sound, like a steel shovel edge hitting rocks in gravel, and he was absolutely covered in unkempt gray hair. It was almost impossible to see his face for the hair, and the lower part of his beard was soaked with tobacco stains from dribbled spit.

"I'm Samuel," Samuel said, "and this is Annie."

Abner nodded and then looked at the dogs, which had

moved in front of the mules and were peering down the trail in the direction of New York.

"Get in the back of the wagon," Abner said.

"What?"

"Get in the back of the wagon. Hide the rifle. Now. Quick. Someone wrong is coming."

"Wrong?"

"Move! Hide the gun!"

Abner's firm voice left no room for argument. Samuel took Annie's hand and they climbed up in the back of the wagon. There was just room for them to sit with their legs out on the opened wagon bed. Samuel hid his rifle and powder horn beneath a pile of cloth.

He had no sooner done this than there was the sound of hooves. A troop of British cavalry dragoons came around the bend in front of the wagon and stopped. Samuel could see through the side of the wagon. There were about twenty riders in red uniforms and high fur hats and knee-high boots. They were carrying short muskets and sabers. The horses were well lathered, snorting and breathing hard, and the group broke formation and spread around the wagon. Two men pulled their sabers and started poking in the load from the sides until Abner said, "Careful there! There's my bairn's bairns inside."

"Your what?" The commanding officer pulled up next to Abner.

"My grandchildren. Don't go poking them with your stickers."

"The purpose of your trip?"

"We're headed for New York. I buy things and sell things. Would you be looking for anything in particular yourself?"

"You could have any kind of illegal goods in there"—the officer nodded at the wagon—"any kind of contraband."

"I could, but I don't. And besides, I have a merchant's pass from the commanding general's staff, handwrit and signed and sealed. All official."

"Let me see it."

Samuel heard the rustle of paper being passed back and forth—he could not see the front of the wagon—and then the officer's brusque voice: "All right then, pass on. But watch for anything suspicious. We've just taken New York and a lot of the rebel runners and deserters are trying to make their way to Philadelphia."

Samuel looked at the troopers around the back of the wagon, who were looking at him. One smiled and nodded at Annie but she sat quietly, her eyes big and her jaw tight.

"Fall in!" the officer commanded, and the men wheeled their horses into formation and rode past.

"Up, Brutus! Up, Jill!" Abner slapped the reins across the rumps of the mules and they grunted and started pulling the wagon, which began to roll ahead slowly.

"Stay in the wagon until they're out of sight," Abner said. "Until they're gone. Then come up on the seat. We'll talk."

Samuel was confused. He'd decided to trust no one and yet this old man had come forward and lied for them. He wasn't sure what to do, but some part of him wanted to trust Abner.

He watched the cavalry unit disappear around a bend in the road and then stood and climbed alongside the load until he was at the seat looking down at the backs of the mules. Annie sat down in the middle next to Abner, and Samuel took the outside.

"How did you know they were . . . wrong?" Samuel asked.

"The dogs. They told me."

"The dogs *told* you?" Annie scoffed. "I didn't hear nothing."

"That's because you don't know how to listen. It's in the way they stand, how their ears set, the hair on their back. If you know the dogs and they know you, they will tell you what to expect."

"How did you know we might think the British soldiers were bad?"

Abner slapped the reins on the mules. "Pick it up, pick it up! How could I think otherwise? Somebody comes down the trail and you hide in the bushes. This is largely a British road. You come out carrying a gun at the ready." He laughed. "It's hard to think you'd act that way with a friend."

"We don't like the British," Annie said suddenly. "They're all bad. Every damn one of them."

They both stared at her. "They killed our folks, our family. . . ." Her voice cracked. "And I miss them. I miss my ma and my pa—I even miss the red chicken that pecked my toes." She started crying, leaning against Samuel.

"I think," Abner said, "you'd better tell me what happened."

And to Samuel's complete surprise, he took a deep breath and did just that.

New York City

New York was the main city where prisoners of the British troops were held. By the end of 1776, there were over five thousand prisoners in New York and, since the population of the city was only twenty-five thousand, more than twenty percent of the people within city limits were captives.

At that time, there was only one prison in New York, so the British held their prisoners in warehouse buildings or on Royal Navy ships anchored in the harbor. Although these ships were built to hold 350 sailors, the British kept over one thousand prisoners at a time on board. The only latrines were buckets, which soon became full and spilled into the prisoners' sleeping quarters.

Disease was rampant. At first, an average of five or six prisoners died on these ships every day. In the end more American soldiers died in prison than in actual combat.

CHAPTER 14

Abner sat silent for a long time after Samuel had finished telling the story of the attack and the raid, although he was less bloody in his telling than he might have been, because Annie was listening.

At length Abner coughed and spit tobacco juice between the mules. "So you're thinking your folks are in New York."

"It's a guess. From what I understand, Philadelphia is in American hands, and I don't think the British would take them there. Caleb heard them talking about going to New York."

"And once you're in New York you're going to find them somehow, and then with your little shooter you're going to lope in there and shoot your way out?"

"Well, no. I mean, I don't know. . . ."

"Right in the middle of the whole British army you're going to sneak in and take them clean away."

"When you put it that way, I guess . . ."

"I heard they had fourteen thousand troops for the battle to take Brooklyn Heights alone; the Continentals never had a chance, started running before the fight started. They've probably got twenty, twenty-five thousand troops swarming all over the area. And you're going to jump in the middle of 'em—it'd be like climbing into a swarm of bees."

"I don't have a plan just yet. All I know is to follow them as best I can and then work on something if I find them. *When* I find them."

"You know what I think?" Abner looked at him.

"No, sir."

"You don't have to call me sir."

"Yes, sir. I mean, no, I don't know what you think."

"I think you need help from an old coot and a couple of dogs, that's what I think."

"You'd do that? Couldn't that land you in a lot of trouble? I mean, you've got that pass that lets you go places—why would you want to help us and risk losing the pass?"

Abner snorted. "Ain't no pass at all. Got a friend in Philadelphia with a printing press, and I had him make me a peck of forms with the date blank and a place for somebody to sign. Official-looking. I just fill in the blank with the right general's name and sign it—works every time."

"That still doesn't answer the question. About helping us." Samuel watched as the dogs moved to the front of the mules, one on either side, looked ahead intently, then dropped back.

"Somebody's coming," Annie said. She'd seen the dogs move. "Shouldn't we stop?"

"Not soldiers," Abner said, shrugging and spitting. "Just people traveling—maybe getting out of New York. Was it soldiers, the dogs would have stayed up front, kept watching."

"How do they know?"

Abner shook his head. "No way to know that unless you're a dog. They kind of feel things, in the air, maybe, or along the ground. Sometimes they'll put their noses down and tell it that way. But they're always right."

And they were right this time. A freight wagon was coming. Not as full as Abner's, and pulled by a team of oxen rather than mules. There was a man walking on one side of the oxen, carrying a wooden staff, which he used to guide them, and a woman walking on the other side. On the wagon seat were two children, probably three and four years old.

They passed head-on and Samuel thought neither of them would say anything. The man just nodded at Abner. But before he was well past, Abner called: "Dragoons ahead, patrolling the road west."

"Thankee," the man said with a nod. "We're obliged for the knowledge, but we're going south at the turn. Head down for Philadelphia, if'n it's still held."

"Held solid. Good journey," Abner said, "for you and the family, and good health."

"The same to you."

And they were gone.

"Why don't the British soldiers come at them? Do they have a pass?"

"Probably not. I doubt anybody really gets a pass like mine. But the soldiers aren't always a problem. Sometimes they take things, act up rough, but other times they seem to follow some kind of rule. Unless they be Hessians. Then even the pass might not work." He shook his head. "They ain't nothing good about the Hessians. They were born bad."

Annie nodded. She had been so quiet Samuel had almost forgotten she was there, sitting between them. Her voice was brittle, like it could break in the middle of a word. "They're all bad."

It will be years, Samuel thought, before she can forget. Maybe her whole life. And I don't blame her—I feel the same and I didn't see my parents bayoneted.

The thought of his parents brought back the memory of the question he had asked Abner, which had not been answered. "We never heard why you want to help us," he said. "Couldn't it make trouble for you?"

"No more'n I make for myself."

"Still."

"You're pushing at this, ain't you?" Abner smiled, though in the hair and spit stains it was hard to tell. "Kind of like a root hog, digging at it."

"I want to know. It doesn't make sense. You don't know anything about us. But you'd risk trouble to help us?

You've got to admit it seems strange—I mean, I'm grateful. Mighty grateful. But . . ."

"Well, thinking on it, there's two reasons."

"We're listening."

"First, when you get old and start to smell an end to things, your brain starts doing things on its own, whether you like it or not. You might be looking at a piece of meat cooking on a fire, hungry and ready to eat, or sitting up here alone, watching the mules pull on a lazy sunny afternoon, and your brain starts in adding and subtracting, measuring your life."

"What do you mean?" Annie looked up at him.

"Well, it says you've done this many things wrong and this many things right. Like a ledger with lines down the middle. Maybe you helped somebody load a wagon once and that would go on the good side, and then maybe you ate a piece of pie somebody else wanted, somebody else deserved, and that would go on the bad side."

"Well, we all do that, don't we?" Samuel asked. "Think about things and then try to do the right one?"

"We can hope so, but until you get old you don't really start adding them up. When you're young you forget some of the things, both good and bad, but when you get old, it's amazing how much you remember. I keep pulling up parts of my life from when I was barely off the milk, bawling after my mum in Scotland. I stole a tiny piece of bread I wasn't supposed to eat on the ship on the way over here, and *that's* in there, waiting to be added in, even though I puked it up not two minutes after I ate it." He snorted and spit, this time almost to the noses of the mules. "I wasn't one for sailing. The boat rocked once, the first time I got on it, and I was sick all the way across."

He stopped the wagon because they met some young men on foot, obviously fleeing. There were three of them and one had bandages around his upper left arm. They waved but kept moving west along the trail at a trot.

Abner warned the men about the cavalry and they nodded. Samuel thought they should be moving off the side of the trail into the brush but didn't say anything. They probably knew more than he did, since they'd been fighting.

He was very glad that he and Annie had run into Abner but knew that if they hadn't, they would have traveled as much as possible in the thick brush. In the woods was life. Out here in the open . . .

"You said two," Samuel said, watching the men until they were out of sight. If the cavalry were coming back they would be caught, probably killed. It all seemed so crazy: men walking down a road, somebody coming along and killing them. "Two reasons to help us. What's the other one?"

"Well, the first one was almost all rubbish. I mean, it's true, but maybe a little too flowery to be real. I like the way it sounds, though, almost like it might be written somewhere." Abner chuckled. "Being alone most of the time, I don't get much chance to flower things up. Maybe

I should write it down. Somebody might read it sometime and think I was more than I really am."

Lord, Samuel thought, for somebody who spends most of his time alone, he sure does like to hear his own voice. He waited.

"But the second is quick. The truth is that I'm too old to fight." Abner laughed; Annie jumped and Samuel realized she'd been dozing. "I like a good scrap and I'm too old for this one. So I go back and forth with news. Try to help."

"You're a spy?"

"No, no, that's too hard a word. Though I 'spect these redcoats would hang me proper if they knew. I go back and forth with news about things that are happening that some might be interested in hearing about. I sell a little and buy a little and carry a word now and then, and I help them that needs it when I can. I can't really fight—my bones would break. But if I help those who are against the redcoats, it's right close to fighting. I can't stand the redcoats and you don't like them, either. Is that good enough for you?"

Samuel nodded, watching the dogs move up the trail and back again. "That's good enough for me. And thank you for the help."

Covert Communication

Both the American and the British military forces disguised their communications so that messages could not be easily read if captured by their enemies. Prearranged letters or words replaced other letters or words, all of which had to be memorized by huge numbers of different people, but the secret codes were frequently and easily broken. Mathematical codes were experimented with, but the complexity limited their effectiveness, especially given the length of time it took to pass messages from one party to another.

Invisible inks that could be made visible with heat or a series of chemicals, as well as messages hidden in common publications such as pamphlets and almanacs, were common ways to ensure the security of sensitive information.

CHAPTER 15

They were still several days away from the city of New York and an almost constant stream of refugees came at them.

Some had obviously been soldiers, or fighting men of one kind or another. There were many with wounds, wrapped in crude bandages. Abner stopped the wagon and furnished bandages for those who didn't have them; he also had a supply of laudanum, a painkiller that was half opium and half alcohol, and he gave some of the more gravely wounded a small bottle. "Take it sparingly," he said in his deep voice, "best at night before sleeping." To everyone he said, "Stay off the roads, redcoats are about."

Cart after wagon after cart passed them, being pulled by mules or oxen. A goodly number of the people were soldiers, but the vast majority were civilians—often whole families.

"Where do you suppose they're all going?" Samuel thought of the devastation on the trail to his rear. It certainly didn't seem like a safe place. Hessians, soldiers, savages. "Down to Philadelphia?"

Abner nodded.

At times travelers were so thick Abner had trouble moving the wagon through.

"Are they running from the redcoats?" This from Annie, who teared up when she saw a little girl trudging along and holding a doll by one arm.

"That. And more," Abner said. "Not just the soldiers—like I said, some of them aren't that bad. I mean, a while ago, we were all loyal Englishmen. It's more what redcoats signify—the English Crown has become a way of life these people no longer want. Part is they're scared, don't know what will happen, but along with that, these people are sick of being told what to do by a crazy king who lives three thousand miles away and doesn't care about them one way or the other."

"What do you mean, 'crazy'?" Samuel asked.

"King George," Abner said, "they say he's teched, crazy as a bag of hazelnuts. They've got people to catch him when he runs wild, put his clothes on when he tears them off, watch him when he sleeps so he doesn't kill himself—he's no man to run a kingdom."

"Did he start the war?" It seemed a logical question; the war was so crazy. Maybe a crazy man started it.

"Probably not. It began on this side of the ocean in

Boston, not over there. People were sick of being treated like livestock."

The dogs had been going ahead now and then to greet some people, their tails wagging, holding back with others, but now they dropped well back and Abner stopped the wagon. "British coming." If he hadn't seen the dogs, he would have known anyway; all the men who looked like patriot soldiers evaporated off the trail into the brush.

The soldiers came marching in a file. Not Hessians but regular British soldiers. There must have been two or three hundred of them, as near as Samuel could estimate, marching in loose route step, followed by supply wagons. They did nothing threatening, they didn't stop at all, except to work around wagons that couldn't get out of the way soon enough.

Abner watched them go by in silence, nodding at some of them, and when they were gone, he started up the mules. It was late in the day and he said, "Why don't we stop for a good meal tonight?"

They had been eating corn and the venison, which was about gone. Samuel had been thinking he should take his rifle and head off into the woods for another deer tomorrow. "What do you mean?"

"I mean have somebody cook us a meal . . . say the people in that farm over there." He pointed to a farm set well back off the road, with neat white fences and a white painted house. "Right there."

Samuel and Annie said nothing. The house reminded Samuel of Annie's home before the Hessians and he wondered if she felt the same.

As they had gotten closer to the city, there had been more and more cleared farms. Some were nice, even beautiful. Some had been attacked and burned—probably by the Hessians—but many had not. It made no sense, nor did it follow any logic—like so much of what had happened.

Abner pulled the wagon into the long drive and then the yard. There was a wooden watering trough by a hand pump and the mules went to it and started drinking. Abner, Samuel and Annie climbed down from the wagon.

"Let them drink," Abner said. "Mules won't blow themselves by overdrinking the way horses do."

There was a barn—painted red, as Caleb's had been. Samuel sneaked a look at Annie, but she seemed to take it in stride.

A man came from the barn. He was tall, thin, and had a tired felt hat, which he pushed to the back of his head. He started to say something but before he could get anything out, Abner held up his hand.

"Name's Abner McDougal. Honor to the house and we come in peace. I have a fine surface-sharpening stone wheel and I repair and sharpen all tools, in the house and barn, all work for one good meal for me and the bairns."

"Well . . ."

"Also buy and sell rags. Have some nice linen rags if the

lady of the house needs some soft garment material." He spoke fast, never letting the man get a word in. "If you don't need anything we've got, we'll just thank you for the water for the mules and be on our way."

The man removed his hat and rubbed his head. "Well, I've got some sickle bars that could use a honing and I 'spect Martha has some knives that need touching up."

"No sooner said than done. Sam, why don't you get that sharpening wheel down and we'll get to edging things up."

Samuel—who had never been called Sam in his life—went to the back of the wagon and peered into the mess. He hadn't really looked at it before but now, as he pulled some things aside, he found a sharpening wheel, a wooden frame with a treadle and a small tin cup to drip water on the stone. When he pulled it out of the way, he found a wire-covered crate pushed under some things. It had some kind of birds in it and on closer examination he saw they were pigeons; live pigeons. How strange.

He hadn't even known they were there. Why were they hidden? He took the wheel down and put it by the trough, filled the tin cup and hung it by the wire over the wheel so water would drip from a small hole in the can onto the stone. He made sure the treadle worked and the wheel spun.

The man came from the barn with three hand sickles that had the long curved blade used for harvesting wheat or other grains. Abner took one, stood by the wheel and gestured to Samuel to start pumping with his leg to get the stone spinning. Abner held the first blade against the stone as it turned, making a scraping-hissing sound, and the steel edge ground down to razor sharpness.

Samuel was amazed at how easily the stone spun. This shouldn't take too long. How peaceful it all seemed. He kept pumping until the sickle was done.

Then another, and Samuel switched pumping legs.

Legs a little tired.

And another. He switched legs again.

Legs a little *more* tired.

Then three axes, two picks, a tomahawk, a set of rail-splitting wedges—six of them—four slaughtering and sticking knives, and four butcher knives that Martha, a short, thin woman who was all smiles, brought from the house. Then an ice chisel, two serrated hay knives, two planking adzes, one shingle froe, and, at last, an old cavalry saber that the farmer—named Micah—used for chopping corn.

Samuel staggered over to the trough to wash. Abner put his whole head underwater and then shook like a dog. He pulled his hair back and combed his beard down and Samuel saw Micah smile at him. He saw something else there, a look of what? Recognition? As if they already knew each other?

The meal was good, very good, though not up to what they had eaten at Caleb's. Venison stew, piles of new potatoes, fresh bread with new butter, apple pie made with maple sugar, and fresh buttermilk cool from the spring-house on the side of the barn, in quantities to fill even Samuel. He was shy about asking for seconds, but Martha kept piling it on and he ate it gratefully. Sit-down meals were always rare in his life, even before the war—he winced at that thought, *before the war;* there didn't seem to be such a thing anymore—what with his living in the woods on the hunt most of the time. But being a guest was almost unheard of and he wasn't sure how to act.

He needn't have worried. As with Caleb and Ma, Micah and Martha made eating enjoyable, not something to fret over. When they were done with seconds, and thirds on the pie—even Annie ate like a wolf—they went out to sit on the porch while Micah and Abner lit up clay pipes with coals from the fireplace.

"Food gets better every time I stop here," Abner said, ending the mystery. "I didn't think it was possible."

"She can cook." Micah nodded, smiling. "In fact, there ain't much she *can't* do."

Annie and Samuel sat on the edge of the porch. The dogs were in the dirt in front of them. Annie was about to doze off but Samuel wanted to listen, so he sat drawing pictures in the dirt with a stick, the dogs watching with a kind of casual interest as the stick moved around.

"Know anything about the happenings in New York?" Abner asked. "How it went?"

Micah shook his head. "Not much. The English took it and a bunch of prisoners. They've moved in, the English.

Took over houses for their own—they ain't making a lot of friends. Course that doesn't seem to bother them much, not making friends, the way they brought those damn Hessians into it. Hiring mad dogs."

"The passes I brought you working out?"

"So far. I'm more worried about scavengers hitting us. The wild ones would kill you for a turnip. But we're still here, ain't we?"

"Good. I've got some more birds to leave. You still have that hutch in back of the barn?"

"Yes."

"Same as before. Send one if anything big comes along. I'll send one this evening. We saw a large detachment heading up the road today—maybe two hundred. They ought to know about it back in Philadelphia."

"If the hawks don't get him. I don't know how any of them get past the hawks."

"Well, there's always that. Always some risk. But it's better than nothing."

The pigeons are for carrying messages, Samuel thought. He glanced at Abner out of the corner of his eye—there was so much more to him than he'd thought at first.

The men sat smoking in silence for a moment; then Abner said: "You said they took some prisoners. Sam's parents weren't military but they took them prisoners anyway."

"They're doing that." Micah nodded. "No sense to it.

Just see a man working in a field and take him prisoner. Stupid. Like they think the crops are going to plant themselves."

"You know where they're keeping the prisoners?"

"Not certain. There are warehouses and an old sugar mill—you remember that three-story thing they built to mill sugar?"

Abner nodded. "Along the waterfront."

"Yes. I think they might use that, along with the warehouses. There are thousands of prisoners. I don't know how they'll feed them, plus I s'pose plenty of them were wounded. It can't be good for them."

"Well," Abner said, knocking his pipe out on the side of the porch. This, Samuel saw, made the dogs stand up and get ready. He was amazed by them. They saw everything. "We'll see what we can see," Abner said. It was starting to get dark. "You mind if we sleep here tonight? We'll be out of here early."

"Why would I mind? There's new hay in the loft, makes a good bed, long as you don't smoke."

And with the mules unharnessed, fed hay and put out in a pen for the night, Abner took time to put two pigeons in the hutch in back of the barn. He wrote something on a tiny piece of thin paper, tied it to a third pigeon's leg and let him go. He and Samuel and Annie watched the bird fly away to the south.

"He'll roost somewhere tonight if he doesn't get there before dark. It's probably only forty miles in a straight flight, an hour the way they move, so he should make it. Imagine, moving through the air at forty miles an hour. Just imagine."

Later, lying on the new hay with the clover smell thick around him, Samuel could hear Annie breathing regularly in sleep. He teetered on the edge of it, but before it came he said to Abner, who was lying just above him on the stacked hay bales: "You and Micah aren't what you seem to be, are you?"

"We are," Abner chuckled, "exactly what we seem to be—and maybe just a little bit more."

Civilian Intelligence

Individuals and civilian spy networks carried out the most vital American intelligence operations of the Revolutionary War. Men and women whose daily lives and work brought them into proximity with the British military, such as farmers and merchants, fed important information to the American authorities throughout the war. Some patriots even posed as loyalists to infiltrate pro-British groups, collecting detailed facts about British military operations and defenses, supply lines and battle plans.

CHAPTER 16

There was a long, shallow hill as they came into what Samuel would have called a city, and Abner stopped the mules at the top of it, still half a mile out, and studied it.

Samuel had never even imagined such a place. Houses and other buildings everywhere, built on the land next to the open water. And that water was another thing he'd never seen. "Is that it?" he asked. "That water—is that part of the ocean?"

"That's the Hudson River," Abner sighed. As they'd moved from settlement to settlement, each one bigger than the last, Samuel and Annie had been asking, "Is this New York?"

"And that's not New York, either," Abner said. "Not yet. We're in New Jersey. Look there, across the river, through the fog—that's New York. We'll leave the wagon here and the mules and get a boat across. I know somebody who might help us."

Down below, on mudflats that led out to the river, Samuel saw dozens of boats pulled up to the shoreline, some large, some small, and men waiting to row them across the river. Now and then through the mist, he could make out what seemed to be a large city.

Large? Huge.

"Wait here," Abner said. "I'm going to go look for a friend."

Between the wagon and the river were many buildings, some with fenced-in pens full of oxen and horses and mules.

Abner came back. "Very well." With him was a man who looked a lot like him: gray hair everywhere, tobacco spit down his chin, old clothes. "Matthew here is going to take us across and bring us back. We have had enterprise with each other before and he understands the nature of our business. I told him we hope it won't take long and that we prefer coming back in the dark, if possible, and fast. We'll leave the wagon and mules and dogs with his boys on this side. They'll keep them ready for us. Samuel, you may take your knife, but leave your rifle here. There are soldiers everywhere and a rifle will draw attention. Annie, you wait here with the wagon."

"No."

"Yes."

"He is all I've got."

"And he will be back. If this works right there will be

two more people coming back with us, and the boat is not that big. We might need the room. . . .”

She looked at Samuel. “You come back.”

“I will.”

“I'm telling you, you better or else.”

Samuel could see that she was crying and he found himself choking up but hid it. “Don't worry.” He put his hand on her shoulder.

The truth was he had no idea . . . about anything. They didn't even know for certain if his parents were over there. He looked across the river. It was late afternoon and the sun was burning the fog off. The city was huge, with buildings standing three and four stories high, and houses spread out in a grid.

How could they hope to find anybody in all those buildings? Looking at the city, imagining how many people must be there, made the rest of the trip seem almost easy. The woods, the forest, was nothing compared to this.

“Away,” Matthew croaked. “We must go. Darkness comes fast on the river and we must be across when there is still light for to see. Follow.”

Abner moved with him toward the boats and after a moment's hesitation Samuel followed. There were about a hundred boats pulled up along the mud bank in a long line, tied to brush or small trees, and most of them looked to be on their last legs. Water-soaked, unpainted clunkers, covered with mud and filth that came down the river. Samuel was surprised—considering that Matthew looked even rougher than Abner—to find that he brought them to a beautifully maintained, painted double-ended boat about twenty feet long. There was a small cabin in the center and a short mast up over the cabin.

The cabin itself could only take two people. Matthew said, "Get inside. What isn't seen isn't noted." He grunted as he heaved the boat out of the mud and into the slow current. Then he jumped in, pulled the sail up—the canvas surprisingly clean and well tended—and stood to the tiller. There were no seats or benches except in the cabin, but a wooden bailing bucket was in the stern. As soon as the boat was moving in the soft breeze, Matthew pulled the bucket over and sat, put a chew of tobacco in the corner of his cheek, smiled through discolored teeth at Samuel and said, "Your ma and pa know you're coming to get 'em?"

Samuel looked sharply at Abner—he must have told Matthew the whole story. Abner smiled. "We have done a mite of business together. I told him what we were doing. You can trust him with your life, which"—he snorted—"is exactly what you're doing."

Abner has a whole network, Samuel thought, to work against the British. People on farms, pigeons, and now the man with this boat. Abner was the most amazing man Samuel had ever met.

"No," Samuel said. "They probably think I'm dead, killed by the Indians."

Matthew nodded. "A fair surprise for them, then. It's good to have surprises for your family."

And he tended to sailing the boat and didn't say another word all the way across the river. It was just as well because with the lack of anything productive to think about—Samuel didn't know where they were going, wasn't sure what he would find, and didn't know what he would do when he found or didn't find his parents—his mind was taken up by the sailing.

The boat must have been fairly heavy, yet it skimmed along over the water like a leaf. It wasn't so terribly fast—maybe three or four miles an hour—but it seemed . . . graceful in some way. No, that wasn't it. Free. The wind moved them along quietly and nobody worked to make it so—it just happened.

The boat nudged into the bank.

"Out," Matthew said. "And up the bank. The road into town is on the left, sugar mill down to the right a quarter mile. I'll come back every night at midnight and wait until three in the morning for four nights. If you're not here by then I'll figure the worst. What do you want done with the girl if you get scragged?"

"Can you take her?" Abner paused. "Into your family?"

Matthew hesitated. "Well," he said, "Emily always wanted a daughter. So be it. But we'll bet against it."

And he pushed the boat back out into the current and was gone.

Abner said, "Let's get to it." And he moved up the bank with Samuel following.

At the top Samuel stopped dead. There were people

everywhere, all along the road into the city and down the side road that led to the sugar mill, maybe hundreds of them, and it seemed that almost every man was wearing a red coat.

Soldiers were wherever you looked, armed and walking next to the buildings, roughly forcing civilians to move out into the street.

"Let's start down toward the mill," Abner said. "There might be somebody we can talk to, get a mite of information."

They hadn't gone twenty yards when two soldiers, rifles fixed with bayonets, stopped them. "State your business," one said.

"I'm on the Crown's business," Abner answered. "From across the river. Looking to bring food to the prisoners. I was told they're in the old sugar mill, is that so?"

The soldiers laughed. "Aye," said one. "There and in warehouses and churches. But don't waste food on the rebels. You might as well feed it to hogs, for all the good it will do. They're all marked for the box."

They went off laughing and Abner started walking again, heading for the sugar mill, Samuel following. What had the soldiers meant by "marked for the box"? He was so engrossed in his thoughts and in keeping up with Abner, who could walk surprisingly fast, that he almost ran full-on into his mother.

His mother.

Right in front of him.

It was a thing that could not happen. Impossible. For the first moment, neither of them believed it.

She was dumping out a bucket of slops in the gutter as he was dashing down the street after Abner. She glanced up at him and then back at the pail, just as he dodged out of her way, hurrying to keep up with Abner.

In that instant, though, their heads jerked back to face each other. And they stood stunned, the world around them stopped.

"Sa . . . Samuel?" She dropped the bucket to the ground, reaching out her hand, cracked and red and worn, to gently touch his cheek. "Are you . . . We thought you were . . . after the attack . . . Is it . . . is it really you?"

Samuel couldn't breathe, couldn't speak. "I . . . We . . ."

And then they were holding each other, both crying, until Abner said:

"Leave off! Dammit, leave off! People are watching. Back away!"

They moved away from each other. She was very thin and drawn and looked so small, Samuel thought. "Father? Is he . . . ?"

"Down the road, in that big building. An old sugar mill, full of men, prisoners. I work in this house"—she pointed—"cleaning. I get a corner to sleep in and leftover and scrap food, which I take to your father each night. I'm a prisoner, too, but this family treats me fairly." She stopped. "What happened to your head?"

"It's nothing."

"It's scarred—"

"Tell us about the prisoners," Abner cut in. "Everything you know."

She looked at Abner, then at Samuel. "He's helping me," Samuel said. "Tell him. Everything."

"Helping you what?"

"We don't have time now, Mother. Tell him what he asks." Samuel worried they'd be caught talking and she'd have to go in. "Please."

"The prisoners are barely fed. Your father can hardly stand or walk."

"Guards," Abner said. "How many guards?"

"There are guards inside with the prisoners. At the door—two. But one sleeps almost all the time. The other is by the main door. The back door is nailed and boarded shut. There's only one way out. If there was a fire—"

"Can you get a private message to your husband? Today or early tonight?"

She nodded. "When I bring the food. The guard goes through it and takes anything good. It's such a small amount, you'd think he'd just let it be. But I will find a way to hide a message."

"Tell him to be at the front door at midnight, at the middle of the night if he hasn't a watch. Tell him to be there hiding close by the guard. Alone. Just him, understand?"

"Yes."

"Can you slip out at midnight?" Abner was abrupt, terse. "Right here, at midnight?"

"I will. There are a lot of drunken soldiers on the street at night. But yes."

"All right. Do that. Tell your husband to get by the door at midnight alone, and you be out here at midnight or just a few minutes after."

She nodded, looking from Abner to Samuel.

"We'll come for you then, if everything works right. Now say your goodbyes and get back in the house before we get discovered."

"Samuel," she said, turning toward him, "you're sure you're all right?"

"Everything will be right after tonight, Mother."

"Please, please, be careful. I thought you were dead and I just got you back. I can't lose you again."

"Go inside," he whispered. He almost smiled. Telling him to be careful now, after all that had happened—that horse was well and truly gone from the barn. "We'll be back later."

They looked at each other. She smiled, her lips trembling, staring at him as if to memorize his face. Then, at last, she picked up the slop bucket and went back into the house.

Prisoners of the British

During the war, at least sixteen British hulks—ships that had been damaged and abandoned—lay in the waters off the shores of New York City as floating prisons. Over ten thousand prisoners died of intentional neglect—starvation and untreated disease. Their bodies were tossed overboard into the harbor or buried in shallow graves at the shoreline by fellow prisoners.

CHAPTER 17

Darkness.

Like the inside of a dead cow. There had been a sliver of a moon but clouds covered it and with them came a soft rain. Enough to make everything wet and uncomfortable outside. A godsend. Even drunken soldiers didn't like to be out in the rain.

Abner and Samuel had gone by the sugar mill just before dark to look it over. Samuel's mother had been right. Only one door was being used and two guards stood there talking. One had a chair. There was a small roof over the entry to keep the rain off.

The building was strangely quiet. If there are hundreds of men packed inside, Samuel thought, there should be more noise. They walked past the guards, who paid them no mind, and down alongside the building. Now and then they could hear scuffling and thumping against the wall on the inside, but nothing else.

When they had walked completely past the building, they crossed the street and came back on the other side. Because of the rain, there weren't many soldiers along the walkways and no one bothered them.

They went along the river to a point close to where Matthew would come across and then moved into some trees along the bank. It was starting to get dark. Abner pulled a small oil-soaked bag from the inside of his coat and took out a watch. "Seven-thirty." He put the watch back, settled down against a tree, hunched up the collar of his coat. "Try to get a little sleep, because later tonight there won't be any."

"How are we going to do it?" Samuel asked. "Get him out?"

"Simple plans are best," Abner said. "Did you see all the bricks around the steps? They probably had more of a porch when the place was new; now the bricks have all fallen down. I'll distract the guard; you take a brick and hit him over the head."

"That's your plan?" Samuel stared at him. "What if both guards are there?"

Abner said, "I'll be ready for him. You just do your part."

Samuel still stared. "We've come this far and you tell me to just hit him over the head with a brick?"

"Hard," Abner added. "Hit him over the head *hard.*

Then we open the door, grab your father and run like hell. Or as fast as we can go. Scoop up your mother, get in the boat, get across the Hudson, hook up the mules, get in the wagon and head out. A good, simple plan."

And in the end that was exactly the way it worked.

Almost.

Samuel surprised himself. After an hour of his thoughts tumbling over each other without sense or reason, in spite of the rain, a veil slipped over his mind and he slept, leaning against the same tree as Abner.

"Let's get to it." Abner shook him awake close to midnight. Samuel rubbed his face and stood.

Abner was gone in the darkness and Samuel had to hurry to catch up. Their path took them past the house where Samuel's mother worked. She was already outside and saw them approach. "I'm coming with you," she said softly as they neared. "To help."

"No. Hold. Hold here. We'll be back," Abner whispered. "Shortly."

As they walked closer to the sugar mill Abner took off his coat and wrapped it so that it seemed he was carrying a bundle. There was a tiny glow from a lantern near the guard, the kind with a small candle inside and a slit to let out a sliver of light.

It was enough for Samuel to see some bricks. He picked one up before they moved within range of the guard.

"Halt!" the guard said as he saw them. Samuel held the brick behind him. "State your purpose."

"Bringing food," Abner said, holding up the bundle, "for the prisoners."

"Advance." The guard stepped forward, interested in the package.

They climbed the steps to the entrance, Abner in front of the guard and Samuel slightly to the side, gripping the brick.

Abner held the bundle out. The guard put the butt of his musket on the ground to free one hand to open the package. He leaned forward and Abner said, in a soft, conversational tone, "Now, Samuel."

And Samuel hit the guard with the brick.

Hard.

A moment's hesitation, then the guard fell. Abner caught him, slid him off to the side of the door, laid him on the platform, turned to the door. "Padlocked." He swore.

Gently, delicately, he worked the keys off the guard's belt and unlocked the door. He flung it open.

Samuel's father was in the doorway and even in the dim glow Samuel could see that he was in bad shape—face skull-like, eyes sunken. He almost fell into Samuel's arms.

But he wasn't alone.

Thirty, forty more men were waiting with him, and as soon as he was outside they piled out, scattering like quail, a stream of prisoners, thin as cadavers, pouring out of the shed in a strange silence, moving off in all directions.

"Come." Abner took Samuel's father's arm. "No time."

With Abner on one side and Samuel on the other, they

carried Samuel's father, toes dragging, through the darkness. Samuel's mother was waiting and hurried over to help. Twice they tripped and stumbled in the darkness, but they were up fast and moved as rapidly as possible to where Matthew would be with the boat.

He wasn't there.

"I'll look up and down the bank," Abner said. "Stay here and watch." He vanished upstream in the darkness. Minutes that seemed like hours passed before he came back.

"Nothing—I'll check downstream."

Again, an interminable time while the three of them stood in silence. Abner came back shaking his head.

"Are you sure Matthew—" Samuel started to ask.

They heard a dull thump in the darkness on the water and then Matthew's voice.

"Here, over here! Caught a crab of wind on the way over that kicked me downstream. Had to tack back up. Here—over here."

They found the boat almost by feel, out in a foot of water. Samuel half-carried his father to the side, and he fell into the boat.

"He needs help," Samuel said. "Get him up and in the cabin—please, help him."

Matthew pulled him into the cabin, then helped Samuel's mother onto the boat and into the cabin as well. Abner jumped in and Matthew pulled up the sail, which filled in the freshening breeze. He said to Samuel: "Push off as you come aboard."

Samuel did so, tripped, flopped into the mud and water, lost the boat and was nearly left behind. In one lunge he caught the gunwale—the boat was picking up speed rapidly—pulled himself up and in, and nearly fell in Abner's lap.

Right then the world ashore went berserk. A gunshot, another; lighted torches could be seen in the vicinity of the sugar mill, carried every which way.

"You didn't," Abner said, "hit him hard enough."

"I thought I killed him!"

"He raised the alarm."

"It matters not at all," Matthew said. "We're away from the light. Torches won't cast out here. Besides, they're looking in all directions."

"A passel of other men came out at the same time. They went all over." Abner sighed and leaned back, resting. "It was good fortune."

"Fortune favors the well prepared," Matthew said. He stood from the bucket, where he was sitting, and took out a package wrapped in cloth. "Emily sent beef sandwiches and milk mixed with rum."

"Rum?" Samuel asked. "Milk and rum?"

"Heats the blood, makes the food go in better. It's not for you, but your father. Here, hand it in the cabin. Tell him to eat slow or he'll lose it."

Samuel took the package and moved into the cabin. If possible it was darker inside than it was outside.

"Mother? Father?"

"Here," his mother said, and he felt a hand on his arm. "Father is next to me."

"I'm here," his father said. "Samuel—I am so thankful to see you." Small laugh. "Well, I can't see you at all. My son, I never dreamed you were still alive, much less that you would win me my freedom in this bold manner." His voice was faint.

"Hold your hand out." Samuel fumbled in the package and pulled out a sandwich. "Matthew brought food."

He held a sandwich out in the void, felt a hand grasp it. He heard his father wolfing it. "Eat slow, or Matthew says you'll lose it." He fished a small lidded crock out of the package. "Here's some warm milk mixed with rum. He says it will make the food go down better."

The chewing slowed as he held the crock out in the darkness, felt his mother's hand take it. "Here," she said, "I've got it. Samuel, who are these men? We owe them so much and we don't even know them."

"They're friends—Abner and Matthew. Matthew owns the boat. We met Abner on the way. We—oh, yes, you have a daughter."

"What?"

"You'll meet her when we get to the wagon. Her name is Annie. She . . . well, she needs us. It's been part of this run." He took a few moments to tell them the part about Annie, without too many details of the Hessian attack. It was too terrible to describe.

"Then she's our daughter," his mother said in a firm voice. "From now on, as good as blood."

His father stopped chewing, swallowed, drank some of the rum-and-milk mixture. "Food. Food. When you haven't had it for a while, it tastes as sweet as anything you've ever eaten. Tell Mr. Matthew thank you."

"You're very welcome," Matthew said from the tiller, which was only six feet away. "I'll tell Emily you like her food."

"Like it? It's life itself."

"Aye."

"I feel guilty, though," Samuel's father whispered. "So many men in that shed, in other sheds. Starving. And I get food."

"It is the way of it," Abner put in from the darkness, "of war. Some get, some don't, some live, some . . . don't. It's the way of it."

"It's bad."

"Yes. It is. But it is our lot now, and we must live it." Abner sighed. "The best we know how."

And with that, there was silence the rest of the way across the river, broken only by the lap of water on the side of the boat.

Treatment of Prisoners of War

Prisoners were given only one cup of water a day belowdecks. The rations, issued only in the morning and only half those received by British soldiers, were largely inedible—leftover food from England that was old, stale and, in many cases, rotten. It was not until the nineteenth century that supplies for captives were expected to be provided by their captors; during the Revolutionary War, their own army, government and families attempted to provide for the prisoners.

CHAPTER 18

When they reached the other side of the river and made their way to Abner's wagon, Samuel found Annie asleep, curled up next to Abner's collies.

"Annie." He touched her shoulder to wake her.

She opened her eyes and threw herself into his arms. He staggered backward under her weight and turned to his parents.

"This is our Annie," he said.

His mother reached out and stroked her hair. "Annie. I always wanted a little girl."

"I had a ma," Annie told her, "but then I didn't." She smiled shyly even as the tears welled in her eyes.

"And now you have a ma again," Samuel's mother whispered through her own tears.

"And a pa," Samuel's father said as he stepped next to her.

Abner cleared his throat and started to hook up the mules in the light of the slit lantern.

"No sentries this side of the river," Matthew said. "Just stay to the main road north for a time." He handed them a cloth bag. "Emily fixed food for you to take. Good fortune to all of you."

"I don't know how to thank you," Samuel's father said. "You men have given us back our lives, restored our family."

"Help when you can," Matthew said. "We all need to help. I will go back to the boat now and across the river again. There might be others I can reach before daylight."

And he was gone, and with him the dim glow from the lantern.

"Here now," Abner said. "Everybody inside the wagon except Samuel. Samuel, you come up and ride with me. We must talk."

With his parents and Annie in the wagon, Samuel felt his way up to the front and climbed up in the seat. In near silence, Abner made a soft clucking sound with his tongue and the mules started pulling the wagon up the road. Even with the uproar across the river there was nothing moving on this side. They progressed in quiet for half an hour or so.

The mules, Samuel saw, had no trouble seeing the road in the darkness—were they like cats? Aside from a bump in a rut now and then, it was comfortable. The rain had let up a bit. Samuel's rifle and powder were inside the wagon, covered, so he had no concern on that level.

"We cannot stay together," Abner said suddenly.

"All right," Samuel said, startled. "But why?"

"Too dangerous. If we were stopped before, I could say you were my grandchildren. Now, with your mother and father here, that won't work. There would be questions and, with them, danger. I'm afraid we'd be taken prisoner, in spite of my passes. So we must separate."

"I understand," Samuel said, nodding, though in the darkness Abner could not see it. "You've already done enough—more than enough. I never thought I would see them again. And you have given them back. Well, thank you."

"We all do what we can do. Now, here's the lay of it. We go three more hours on this road. It will get light in four hours. We'll be back in forest, or almost, at that time. Enough for you to have cover. You leave me then and take the forest straight west for two, maybe three hours—your father will be slow for a time.

"There you will come on a large swamp. Just before you get into it, turn left and go southwest toward Philadelphia. It's safe there. You'll be about seven days' travel from town. Here, take this." He handed Samuel something in the darkness, a small brass object like a watch. "A compass."

"Don't you need it?"

"Take it."

"Thank you again."

"Southwest," Abner repeated. "Seven days' walking, maybe eight. It's near on ninety miles to Philadelphia and you'll find trails to help you along. As your father gets stronger you'll move better."

Samuel sat in silence, thinking.

"That's the good news," Abner said. "Now for the bad. Somewhere along there—nobody seems to know exactly where, although it was thought to be down in Trenton for a time—there will be a place where the British have a defensive line. You might not even know you're going through it—but you may run into the redcoats. They'll be a mite jumpy and will probably shoot before talking, so avoid them if you can. If you see them at all. Stay straight southwest, don't fall toward the south over by the main road—that's where they'll be."

Southwest. Samuel was silent, memorizing Abner's instructions. Then he said, "Thank you. There aren't words to—"

"I said that's enough. Now, I don't know what Matthew's Emily put up for food, but try to get something with a lot of fat into your father. Fat is where the power is, red meat and fat. Maybe some raccoon or, if you can, a bear along the way. Thick meat. It's going to be hard for him to walk ninety miles. Be patient."

Again, Samuel nodded. "Yes. I will."

"And with your mother, too. She's very strong but this is different. They're going to try to be your ma and pa, but for now, you have to be the leader. They don't have the knowledge for what's coming. You do. And one more thing: Take an extra blanket."

And then silence, except for the sound of the mules clopping along, and their breathing.

They met no one, or at least didn't see anybody in the pitch-darkness. After a time Samuel realized he could make out the white markings on the dogs. About then Abner pulled the mules to a stop.

"Out here," he said. "Remember, west to the swamp and then southwest."

"Yes. And again, thank—"

"Enough. Away."

Samuel jumped off the wagon and went around to the back. In the dim light he motioned to them to get out. Annie came out of the back half-asleep. Samuel found the food, two bundles, and he gave one to his mother and the other to Annie. Next he tied a blanket to his bedroll and put it over his shoulder; then he located his rifle and powder horn, checked the priming in the quarter-light and found it to be good. As soon as he said, "All right," Abner clucked at the mules and in a moment was gone in the morning mist.

"We didn't get to say thank you," his mother said.

"We can't talk now," Samuel said. "Later. Now we have to get moving. Are you all right to walk, Father?"

"Yes. Maybe a little slow. We'll see."

"Good. Follow me. And again, we can't talk."

He set off without really thinking. He'd been away from the woods and sitting in the wagon for days, out of his element. His body was sick of it, wanted to move, to *move,* and he took off at a near lope.

Annie held the pace, as she had when they'd been traveling together before, but within thirty yards his father gasped, "Samuel, I can't. . . ." His mother was out of breath and limping, but she didn't complain and tried to help support his father.

Samuel slowed then, but he wanted to be well away from the road before stopping, so he kept them moving for over a mile. The sun was near enough to the horizon then to shed light everywhere, even through the clouds. He stopped in a small clearing, unrolled his bedroll and took out the moccasins he had made those days sitting in the wagon. "Father, try these on," he whispered.

"Can we talk now?" his mother also whispered, but he shook his head.

"Not yet. Two more hours." He continued whispering, "Annie, I will walk in front, you in the rear. If I stop, we all stop. Not a sound. If I go down, you all go down—again, not a sound. Annie, every forty or fifty paces you turn and listen with your hands cupped to your ears. If you hear something strange or that bothers you, whistle softly. Then we all stop. Is all that clear?"

"Yes—" his mother started, but he put a finger to her lips.

"We are still in danger, great danger. Please, for now just do as I say."

She smiled at him and rested her hand on Annie's shoulder. He turned to his father. "Can you hold a slow pace for two or three hours?"

His father nodded. "I'll do it."

"Then we go."

Samuel started off, this time at a much slower pace, and as quietly as possible, moving along game trails when he found them, below the tops of ridges if there were any so they wouldn't be silhouetted against the skyline. Stopping every forty or fifty paces for Annie—and Samuel—and to listen, to watch, to know, to *know* if anyone was following them.

His parents and Annie obeyed him and they moved, if not rapidly, at least steadily until Samuel looked down and saw water seeping into his footsteps. The edge of a swamp lay ahead of him.

He found another clearing on slightly higher and drier ground, and let everybody sit while he dug food out of one of the packages. It was slabs of venison—but with little fat—and corn dodgers: corn bread made into small muffins. They had some lard in them, but not much. He fed the others and pretended to eat, but put it back. There was still a long way to go and unless he killed something, they would need all the food they could save.

"All right." He spoke low, almost in a whisper. "A short rest, just a few minutes. Then we start southwest. Ask questions now, but soft."

"What happened to your head?" his father asked. "That scar?"

"I was hit with a tomahawk . . . ," he started, then

realized he'd have to tell the whole story. He did so, leaving out the worst parts.

"We saw you! We saw you!" his mother said. "On the other side of the clearing when the shooting started. It was too far away for us to know it was you, but we saw you when you shot. Did you . . . did you hit . . ."

He nodded. "I fired, he went down, the second one clubbed me and I went down. All very fast."

Then he told of Cooper and the other volunteers who had helped him, leaving out the part about the man screaming for days. He worked past the rest of it—telling about Caleb and Ma, leaving out the Hessians—to the present.

"But how could you . . . ," his father started. "You're thirteen!"

"We'll have time for me to answer everything later. But now let me tell you what Abner said," and he told of the British line they might have to cross, the possible danger, the situation in Philadelphia. When he was done he stood and picked up his rifle. "We go again now, all day if we can. Father?"

"If we go slowly I think it will be all right."

"Drink as much water as you can from each stream. The water helps." And he didn't add that water keeps the stomach full and so less hungry. "Annie, you're in back, me in front. No talking. A soft whistle."

And he set out. He knew his father was weak but he worried that if they favored the weakness, it could get worse. He kept the pace all day, checking the compass every few minutes. They stopped often to drink from the small streams and creeks—and there were many—with short, silent breaks every hour and a half or so, until it was early evening, and he saw his father weaving.

They came to a small rise out of the moist lowlands and he pulled up there, on the back or western side, and stopped.

"No fire," he said softly. "Cold camp. Father, you eat until you're full. Mother and Annie, hold it down to a little, just a taste. I'm going to go check the back trail. Wait here for me."

He trotted back the way they had come, stopping often to listen, smell, absorb. He didn't feel completely safe until he had gone half a mile and had not seen or heard anything. Then he moved back to where he'd left them and found them sitting back against trees, his father and Annie wrapped in his blanket roll, already dozing.

"We're clear," he whispered to his mother, his rifle across his lap. "Get some sleep."

She was studying him. "You're so different. Grown."

"No. I'm the same. It's everything else that's changed."

She shook her head. "No. You've changed. Not in a bad way. You . . . know things. See differently. Think differently. If I didn't know you, I don't think I would recognize you. It's like you've gone to some far place and come back a different person. But I love the new Samuel as much as I loved the old. And I'm very glad, I'm so thankful, that you're with us, to show us, to lead us." She held his hand.

"Good night, Mother."

"Good night, New Samuel."

British Behavior

The British, on their military tear through the countryside as they tried to regain control of the wayward colonists, adopted what later became known as a "fire and sword" strategy rather than a "hearts and minds" policy. That is, rather than attempting to placate and persuade the rebels, they destroyed towns and warehouses; they sacked and burned plantations, crops and livestock; they plundered and stole from households and stores alike without regard to law or justice or the well-being of the people they encountered.

CHAPTER 19

They slept fitfully that first night, especially Samuel. He could not get over the feeling that somebody was following them.

The next day the feeling abated somewhat, but by evening Samuel saw that his father was sliding back a bit. The food Emily had sent was good, but his father needed fat meat. Samuel decided to do a quick evening hunt for raccoon. One shot, hopefully away to the west, was all he would allow himself. With luck, nobody would hear it. They were walking southwest in marshy country, perfect for coon, and he saw tracks all over the place.

He left the group resting and moved to the west an eighth of a mile, walk-hunting, and hadn't gone fifty yards before he saw a small female with two kits. That wasn't what he wanted and he kept going, out from her in circles. Within twenty minutes he came on what he was looking for: a large boar coon halfway up a tall oak, sitting on a side branch.

He moved east of the coon so the sound would go west into the forest, aimed carefully and took him in the head, so that the animal fell backward off the limb, dead when he hit the ground.

Samuel gutted him quickly and left the entrails for scavengers. Some people ate coon liver, he knew, and bear liver—bear and raccoon meat were similar—but he never trusted it. An old man had once told him, "Bear and coon liver will give you the gut gripes," so he stayed away from it.

Back with the others, he skinned the coon, built a small, very small, fire with the driest wood he could locate and cooked the meat in half-pound chunks, fat dripping from it. He killed the fire as soon as the meat was cooked. He forced his father to eat several helpings of it; then he and his mother and Annie ate until they were full. He saved the rest for his father to eat over the next two or three days.

They wanted to talk then, especially Annie, who was nearly bursting. "My talker is about to blow up," she told him. But he shook his head, wiped the grease off his mouth, took his rifle and went back up the trail a quarter mile. He sat in a small stand of hazel brush next to the trail, dozing all night, watching. The sound of the gunshot worried him immensely, as did the smell of smoke from the fire—even a soft breeze could carry the odor of smoke for miles.

But he needn't have worried. Nobody came along and he went back to the family at dawn and awakened them. After letting them tend to themselves in the woods, since there were no privies, he started moving, again, in silence.

That day they stopped for breaks four times and he forced his father to eat more coon. The rest of them ate the remainder of Emily's venison and corn dodgers. They started to hit cross trails about midday.

There was still good forest all around them and they walked in a beautiful green tunnel, although the trail seemed to get more beaten down as they moved southwest. Now and again, they came to cross trails that ran east-west and they went west. These trails were even more compacted, and twice they crossed over paths with twin ruts where carts and wagons had moved through.

These frightened Samuel. They were so wide and exposed that he was especially cautious in the way he let his family cross them. He stood and waited for ten, twenty, thirty beats, listening, then sent one person across at a run, waiting and listening for another long stretch before sending the next person and the next and then, finally, himself.

Which made it all the more difficult to believe when after all that care he got caught.

On day four—even at the slow pace, Samuel thought they had made close to fifteen miles a day—they came into an area that seemed slightly more civilized. Forest, still, but here and there a farm off to the east. They had to bear west to avoid the larger cleared areas.

The cross trails were becoming more substantial as well, double-rutted roads appearing fairly often and, now and then, proper roads—well traveled, hand-graded and planked over the muddy spots.

They came on such a road near the end of the fourth day. It was sunny, although nearly evening, and they had relaxed, knowing they would soon stop for the night. Samuel came around a tight turn in the trail and stepped out onto a real road without thinking.

He was two feet away from the rear end of a British cavalry horse. Samuel froze. The man on the horse, an officer, was looking into the brush on the other side of the road, as was his horse, both ears cocked.

The officer had his saber drawn, held down at his side at a slight angle. Ready.

To his left were five more men on horses, all facing the same way, staring intently, short muskets at the ready, their sabers still in the scabbards.

A second, two, and they still hadn't seen Samuel. The picture would be frozen in his mind for the rest of his life: a split second when everything was still, sane, controlled, nobody hurt, nobody dead; all sitting on their horses, all staring at the other side of the road, all alive, and then, and then . . . chaos.

One man, young, with rosy cheeks, caught sight of Samuel and turned. His mouth opened, he called, started to aim his musket at Samuel at the same instant that Samuel raised his rifle, cocking the hammer. But before he could shoot, or the soldier could shoot, the officer wheeled his horse, which knocked Samuel away, and chopped his saber down at Samuel just as Samuel pulled the trigger on his rifle, aiming up at the officer, the ball taking the man just beneath the chin, killing him instantly as the saber barely caught the edge of Samuel's shoulder. Samuel fell back to see his father coming out of the woods to help him.

"No!" he said as the other soldiers swung their muskets around, when, like thunder, like the very voice of the god of war gone mad, the other side of the road erupted in a shattering roar of flame and smoke. The men on the horses were blown off their mounts into the brush.

Dead. By rebel fire.

Two horses were hit, screaming, staggering back into the brush. Samuel leaned back on his father's arm and, without thinking, reloaded.

The rebels reloaded, followed the redcoats off the road where they had fled, and killed the wounded horses.

Then silence as about fifteen men came out of the brush and checked the British dead for papers.

Samuel tried not to look at the officer he had killed. As with the Indian, it had happened by reflex. So quick. And final.

The death bothered him, but when he thought of that saber coming down at him, he knew there had been no choice.

A soldier in a blue Continental uniform came up to

him. "I'm Sergeant Whitby. We're from the Thirtieth Foot, out of Philadelphia. And you?"

Samuel pointed with a vague wave to his rear, where Mother and Annie came out of the brush to stand by Father.

Samuel couldn't talk—he kept staring at the dead officer, whose hat had come off. The man had long brown hair that waved in the light breeze near the ground. It's like he's still alive, Samuel thought; like that part of him is still not dead somehow. Maybe I didn't really . . .

Samuel's father cleared his throat. "We're—refugees. Trying to get to Philadelphia and safety. My wife and I were prisoners in New York and my son, Samuel, rescued us. This is our daughter, Annie. May we walk with you?"

"Sir, we can do better than that." Sergeant Whitby turned to his troop. "Peters, Donaldson, gather up those four horses. Put this man and his wife and little girl on three horses and all the rest of the equipment, muskets and sabers, on the other. The rest of you get these bodies off the road." He turned back to Samuel's father. "We were sent to set up an ambuscade and take a prisoner or two to find out the situation in New York. Since you came from there I'm going to consider the mission accomplished—you tell us what you know—and there's no reason you can't ride in comfort." He turned to Samuel, smiled and said, "I take it you have no objections to walking?"

Samuel shook his head, then watched the soldiers drag the officer's body back into the brush with the rest, load the horses and start back down the road toward Philadelphia.

Toward safety.

But Samuel hung back, leaning on his rifle, watching them until they were out of sight around a bend.

It was over now, he knew. The run, the madness, listening to every crack of a twig, worrying over every brush of a leaf. His parents and Annie would be safe now. A great weight came off him then and he thought, No, *we* will be safe now.

It's over.

But still he hung there, hesitant to go, to follow, until a young soldier came trotting back and waved at him to come.

He nodded, picked up his rifle and jogged to catch up.

It was over.

Epilogue

He stood leaning on his rifle, on the high ground where he had first seen the smoke from the attack on the settlement.

Three years had passed.

They had settled in Philadelphia and safety. The frontier would never be the same for his parents; the forest would always threaten them. So they had found a house, two stories of wood frame, among the many vacant houses in Philadelphia. Samuel's parents had started a school to take in and teach some of the many children orphaned by the war. Annie had become a great help.

But Samuel had trouble fitting in.

Too much city, too much town, too many people, for him to feel settled, calm; and then there was that other thing that kept bothering him.

The back trail.

After a few months in the city, he told his parents, "Everybody helped us; at great risk they helped us, helped me. Everybody back there gave us everything they had—I have to go back. I owe."

There were arguments, of course, almost outright fighting, that went on for nearly two weeks, but in the end—surprisingly—it was his mother who stopped it. "No," she said finally. "He's right. He may be only sixteen, but age doesn't matter now. He's his own man and if he feels that strong, he must do it."

And, after he sat and talked with Annie and promised he would come back, made a sacred promise that he would come back, she agreed to stay, and let him leave.

And he went back to the war.

He worked his way up to Boston and joined Morgan's Rifles, where he also found Coop and some of the other men who had rescued him. He stayed with them for nearly three years. He saw fighting as he'd never seen it before, but he did not join in the firing; instead he hunted for meat, fixed equipment, helped the sick and wounded as best he could. He stayed until Coop died, streaming with dysentery over a slit trench in an agony of jabbering delirium, killed by dehydration. At the end, Coop didn't even know where he was, didn't know his own name.

Samuel left then.

He went back, but not to Philadelphia, not yet. He went back to the healing forest, where it had all started for him, and where the war had nearly vanished by this time. He found the clearing back in the woods that he had seen that first day, when he'd gone so far from home hunting bear. He stood there, trying to make the last three years not be.

Thinking at last it was over.

But, of course, it wasn't finished.

Philadelphia would be briefly taken by the British. Samuel's parents did not leave, but stayed to help the children. This time, oddly, the British treated them with great kindness; brought them food and blankets.

Thousands more men would be killed, dying from bullets, bayonets and sickness. The world would bring the war to the oceans and naval men would die horribly at sea; France would send troops to help the American colonies, getting so deeply involved that it would destroy the French economy, weaken the government and contribute to causing the French Revolution, in which many of the leaders who had helped America would die, beheaded on guillotines. The madness didn't end. Perhaps it has never ended.

But for Samuel, it would come to a close in the soft beauty of the forest. The peace, for him, would hold.

Afterword

Woods Runner is not an attempt to write the history of the War for Independence. Rather, this book, along with being the story of Samuel and his parents and their part in the war, is meant to clarify some aspects of that conflict that have often been brushed over.

Some of the dreadful nuts and bolts of battle, the real and horrible truths, are frequently overlooked because other parts are more dramatic and appealing. There is a tendency to clean up the tales of war to make them more palatable, focusing on rousing stories of heroism and stirring examples of patriotism, all clean, pristine, antiseptic.

But the simple fact is that all combat is outrageous—thousands and thousands of young soldiers die horrible, painful deaths lying in their own filth, alone and far from home, weak and hallucinating, forgotten and lost.

The Revolutionary War lasted for eight long slaughtering years. Over two hundred thousand men between the ages of sixteen and twenty-five answered the call in the War for Independence and stood to.

Stood to when that often meant death.

Approximately 4,400 young men were killed in combat—by a musket ball, exploding artillery, grapeshot from a cannon, or a steel bayonet shoved through their bodies.

Disease accounts for another thirty to fifty thousand losses. Although it is difficult to determine accurately the number of wounded men who subsequently died of infection, estimates put the figure between fifteen and thirty thousand. Open wounds were bathed with dirty sponges kept in pails of filthy, bloody water. Surgeons went days between washing their hands or instruments. Most of the wounded, seething with dirt, bacteria and infection, were sent home to die months later, well past any documented casualty roll.

The total figure might be on the order of sixty thousand deaths.

Although accurate records of the wounded never existed, the figure is generally thought to be about four wounded for every man who died on the battlefield or died of disease in the camps.

Back then, however, most of the wounded did not live, and so the proportion was more like two wounded for every man killed.

That puts the total casualty figure, conservatively, at a

staggering 100,000 to 110,000. Out of just over 200,000 men who fought, at least half of them died.

In the eastern colonies, whole towns were denuded of young men; they sent their sons and fathers and husbands off and never saw them again, not even to bury them.

The men fighting, and dying, in the War for Independence were, for the most part, average young workingmen with little or no military training. They were fighting the most powerful nation on earth. And they suffered those horrendous casualty rates for an appalling eight years. That these young men and boys stood to as they did, in the face of withering odds, and actually won and created a new country with their blood, is nothing short of astonishing.

About the Author

Gary Paulsen is the distinguished author of many critically acclaimed books for young people, including three Newbery Honor books: *The Winter Room, Hatchet,* and *Dogsong.* His novel *The Haymeadow* received the Western Writers of America Golden Spur Award. Among his Random House books are *Notes from the Dog; Mudshark; Lawn Boy; The Legend of Bass Reeves; The Amazing Life of Birds; The Time Hackers; Molly McGinty Has a Really Good Day; The Quilt* (a companion to *Alida's Song* and *The Cookcamp*); *The Glass Café; How Angel Peterson Got His Name; Guts: The True Stories Behind* Hatchet *and the Brian Books; The Beet Fields; Soldier's Heart; Brian's Return, Brian's Winter,* and *Brian's Hunt* (companions to *Hatchet*); *Father Water, Mother Woods;* and five books about Francis Tucket's adventures in the Old West. Gary Paulsen has also published fiction and nonfiction for adults, as well as picture books illustrated by his wife, the painter Ruth Wright Paulsen. Their most recent book is *Canoe Days.* The Paulsens live in Alaska, in New Mexico, and on the Pacific Ocean.

You can visit the author at www.garypaulsen.com.